I0606642

ROUGH AND TUMBLE

A THRESHOLD SERIES PREQUEL
BY CHRISTA KINDE

Rough and Tumble
a Threshold Series prequel

Copyright © 2015 by Christa Kinde | ChristaKinde.com
ISBN: 978-1-63123-039-4

Cover Art by Anna Earley | AnnaEarley.com

*"No Guardian can keep his composure when
meeting the one he was created to love."*

Introduction

Rough and Tumble is a small story with small chapters, set in the same small town where the Threshold Series takes place. In *The Blue Door*, Prissie Pomeroy gets the barest glimpse of an invisible realm where the Faithful are at war with the Fallen. With *Rough and Tumble*, the point of view tilts into the heavenlies, and the story is told from a very different perspective.

Meet Ethan, the newest angel in the Hedge surrounding the Pomeroy family farm. He's the guardian angel Sent to watch over Prissie's little brother Zeke. *Rough and Tumble* was originally serialized on my blog, with new chapters updating weekdaily. Short and sweet, each installment is exactly 100 words long. A creative challenge for me, a little lift for readers who find their way onto my website.

The timeline for this serial overlaps other books and stories I've written about the Pomeroys. Cameos and cross-references abound. New details are revealed. Future storylines are foreshadowed. The Threshold Series is complete in four volumes, and there are three free short stories available for download. You'll find more details and summaries at the end of the book. And as always, I chat about my latest authorial news at ChristaKinde.com.

But for now, follow one little boy's adventures as he turns his guardian angel's life upside down.

CHRISTA KINDE

1

WAITING IN THE WINGS

Alanky adolescent with light brown bristles for hair bit his lip and tried to figure out where he'd gone wrong. Caramel brown eyes narrowed in concentration as he backtracked.

In his opinion, the hardest part of training was tying bootlaces. The crisscrossing straps might have kept him from flying right out of his footgear, but it always took him three tries to get the pattern right. "Maybe if I was a Weaver, it would make more sense," he mumbled.

"Complaining?" asked a sharp voice.

"Merely clumsy," the youth replied, glancing sheepishly at his mentor. "Am I late?"

"As usual."

2
GUARDIAN IN TRAINING

The pair hurried along streets lined with racks of billowing fabric. All around them, the *click* and *clack* of many looms proved that the Weavers were as industrious as ever. "Your sense of timing needs work," said his mentor. "A Guardian can't afford to be late."

"Yes, Conrad," Ethan replied meekly. They'd been together for a handful of decades, but he was still in awe of the older angel, whose shock of wiry hair was as black as his eyes. Conrad's strength was impressive, and his skill with the sword was inspiring.

"Aerial maneuvers today."

"My opponent?"

Conrad smirked. "Me."

Iron Sharpens Iron

On the very edge of the Weavers' district where the Guardian trainees were quartered stood a small, circular pavilion. A ring of golden stone was set into its floor, and as Conrad hopped lightly onto its rim, he unfurled his wings, shaking them out in preparation for flight. Shifting patterns of violet and red light rustled musically as he waved his apprentice closer.

"Draw your sword *before* you follow," Conrad instructed before dropping out of sight.

Gathering his courage, Ethan extended wings that shimmered in pearlescent shades of pink, drew his blade, and then leapt from the threshold of heaven.

4
GLAD TIDINGS

There were three kinds of Guardians within the ranks of heaven—those who were serving their purpose, those who had fulfilled their purpose, and those whose purpose remained to be seen. Like all the other apprentices in the encampment, the angel with bristle-brush hair learned all he could from his mentor, gaining strength and garnering wisdom while awaiting his call to service by God.

When it came, he felt certain it was too soon. Many others had waited longer; many more were better equipped. Yet there was no mistaking the voice that filled his heart with awe.

'Ethan, it is time.'

TWO BY TWO

"Conrad!" Ethan yelped, nearly tripping over his own feet as he searched for his mentor. He found the tall Guardian on the edge of the practice field, speaking with some of the other angels who'd been given apprentices. "I … I am …!" he began, fumbling for words to express the enormity of his news.

Black eyes flashed with concern, surprise, then utter delight. "Sent?" he prompted.

Ethan nodded shakily.

Conrad broke into a rare smile and pulled his trembling apprentice into a hearty embrace and said, "Don't fret, Guardian. We go together."

The reminder calmed Ethan, who admitted, "I am glad."

6
A Reason for Rejoicing

Word spread quickly, and all the Guardians paused to celebrate the young apprentice's assignment. Within the ranks of the Faithful, there was no envy; their chances would come when the time was right. Conrad's warm baritone rose first, and others quickly joined as the whole encampment blended their voices in a hymn of thanksgiving for the new life that would be under their comrade's watch-care.

Delight suffused Ethan's heart and mind, and when the swell of joy grew too bright to contain, he mingled his light tenor with the gathering song, offering gratitude to God for this chance to serve.

BAREFOOT BOY

Ethan sprawled upon a low wall in a quiet corner of the Weavers' District, basking in the light of heaven. He and his mentor would soon be leaving, and he would miss walking in its radiance.

"Here you are," Conrad sighed. "And out of uniform, no less."

With a sheepish smile, Ethan sat up and wriggled his toes. "I will go get my boots."

Shaking his head, his mentor announced, "Our new captain is waiting. You'll have to come as you are."

Ethan ducked his head. "Am I late?"

"As usual," Conrad replied, giving his apprentice's shoulder a fond cuff.

8
FLIGHT ASSIGNMENT

Ill-equipped and ill-at-ease, Ethan padded after Conrad. Meeting new people always made him nervous, but he *was* curious about his new captain. "Have you met him?" he quizzed his mentor.

"I have. We're assigned to a Protector named Tycho."

"A cherub," said Ethan.

"From the sound of it, we'll see our fair share of them," Conrad said with a chuckle.

"Why?"

His mentor's black eyes glittered. "We're entering a battle Flight—eight Protectors, two Messengers, and us."

"Sounds dangerous."

"Sounds *safe*."

The young Guardian blinked, then smiled. Conrad was good at turning things around so he saw them in new ways.

OH, CAPTAIN, MY CAPTAIN

Tycho was tall and slender with long, wheat-colored hair pulled up into a high ponytail. Piercing blue-green eyes frankly assessed the pair entering the tent. Caught staring, Ethan bashfully lowered his gaze to contemplate his toes.

"Well met, Guardians," Tycho greeted with polite formality. "Your names have come under my hand."

"I'm Conrad, and this is Ethan."

"I must confess," said their captain, "you are the first *hadarim* ever given into my care."

"We're servants of God, the same as you," said Conrad.

"And now, we shall serve together." Tycho offered a thin smile. "Your responsibility has become my responsibility."

10
BOWSTRINGS

"You are an archer?" asked Ethan, his eyes trained on the weapon riding between the slender angel's shoulders.

"I am." Tycho brought his bow around and held it out on his palms, displaying the intricate carvings on its grip. "Come and see."

Ethan drifted closer and studied the beautiful craftsmanship. Letters had been worked into the decorative pattern. He soon found his name listed along with those of the other angels under Tycho's watch-care. "When will I meet these angels?"

"We leave immediately." With a brief glance at Ethan's bare feet, Tycho's tones betrayed hints of amusement. "Or shortly thereafter."

MATCHED SET

Tycho led Conrad and Ethan to a jumping-off point near one of the cherubim Enclaves. A pair of Protectors awaited them.

"Our escort," their captain explained.

Ethan stared back and forth between the two, for the bowmen were virtually identical. Both had tanned skin, and brown hair hung in thick braids down their backs. Violet eyes echoed the plummy hues in their wings.

They swapped knowing looks and broke into grins that revealed matching dimples.

"I'm Garrick," announced one, tapping his ear cuff meaningfully. "Mentor to Yannis here."

Yannis gave his bare ear a playful tug. "Welcome to the Flight!"

12
DOPPELGANGER

"**A**re you twins?" asked Ethan. Their resemblance was uncanny … and confusing.

"You'd think so, to look at us," replied Yannis, shifting his wings to catch currents. "I've heard that twins are *possible*, but we're not."

"I'm much older," Garrick explained.

Yannis nodded. "He's a First One, but I was formed two centuries ago."

Garrick's dimple deepened. "Those in our Flight say Yannis has learned his lessons *too* well. Mentor and apprentice have become indistinguishable."

Ethan smiled shyly. "There is something pleasing in symmetry."

Yannis grinned more broadly. "And above all else, we live for the good pleasure of God."

13

An Encampment of Angels

Time dragged at Ethan's wings as the five angels banked into a swiftly-dropping spiral. He spotted a white stone tower gleaming in the moonlight far below. At Tycho's sharp command, he and Conrad drew their swords, for the enemy would pick off the unwary.

Passing through the ranks of an angelic host, Ethan's sandals touched earth for the first time, and he gazed curiously at the neat rows of tents arrayed around the base of the tower.

"Our encampment," Tycho explained.

"There must be a whole legion!" Ethan exclaimed.

"*Two* legions," corrected Tycho. "Come, meet the rest of your teammates."

14
Home Away from Home

Tycho led them into a roomy tent hung with tapestries that testified to the incredible skills of the Weavers. The space was crowded with various necessities. Armor stands, spare quivers, and bundles of arrows lined the perimeter. Tables were strewn with bowstrings, bootlaces, and battle plans.

"This is where our Flight gathers to eat, rest, and recover," Tycho explained.

Ethan noticed a measure of manna, a lap harp, and rolls of bandages. He wondered about the angels they belonged to.

"The others will arrive after the second watch to share a song."

Conrad thumped Ethan's back. "His first true evensong."

15

TYCHO'S FLIGHT

The assembled cherubim all seemed older, wiser, and bolder than Ethan. He hardly knew how to respond to all their promises to watch out for him.

Tycho smiled faintly and explained, "We are Protectors; it is what we do."

As the tent grew noisy, Ethan faded into the background, only to bump into someone just entering.

The angular teen had pale skin and powder-puff black hair. Green eyes widened in surprise, but he looped an arm around Ethan's shoulders. "Hiya! I'm Raz, apprentice Messenger."

"We are teammates?"

"Yep!" Raz confirmed. "But we can do better than that! Let's be *friends*!"

16
THE MESSENGER'S APPRENTICE

Of all the angelic orders that Ethan had encountered, Messengers were his favorites. They were so friendly, and their uncanny ability to carry on one-sided conversations made things simpler for a tongue-tied Guardian like himself.

When evensong concluded, Raz nudged his shoulder and asked, "Are you excited?"

"In part."

"Nervous?"

"A little," Ethan admitted.

"Yesterday, I was Sent ahead to meet the Guardians in your Hedge," Raz revealed. "Those guys will lend a hand if you need it, and Conrad knows what's what. Plus, you'll see *me* every day!"

"I will?"

"Yep. I'm the one assigned to bring your meals!"

"**W**hat can you tell us about our placement?" Conrad inquired as they winged away from the encampment.

Raz zoomed through a loop-the-loop, fairly bursting with excitement. "If I were you, I'd be thanking God, for His grace falls richly on this family."

Conrad's alert eyes snapped to the young Messenger's face. "They are believers?"

"Jayce and Naomi already have four children, and those little ones are being raised in the nurture and admonition of the Lord," Raz confirmed.

Filled with awe, Ethan whispered, "Can we hurry?"

"No need." Raz pointed toward a sprawling farm surrounded by fruit trees. "We're here!"

18
HEDGE OF PROTECTION

Conrad swung into a wide circle over the farm, and Ethan kept close.

"This is a good place for setting up a defense," Conrad announced. "The boundaries are clear, and the Hedge is strong."

Ethan peered curiously at the sprawling acreage below, picking out the bright splashes of color that showed where more than a dozen other hadarim were stationed. When a group of Guardians served together in one location, they were referred to as a Hedge.

"As you can see, the Pomeroys grow apples," Raz said conversationally, pointing eastward. "Their orchard stretches from here to the front lines."

THE FARMHOUSE KITCHEN

The house was blanketed in a sleepy hush, for dawn had not yet touched the eastern sky. Striding confidently into the kitchen, Raz gestured for them to take seats at the huge table. "I'll let Lucan know he has company!"

Moments later, a fierce-looking warrior entered. His hair stood out in wild corkscrews, and matched sword hilts rose above broad shoulders. He regarded them with silver eyes that contrasted starkly with ebony skin.

Ethan fidgeted under this Guardian's scrutiny.

Then, understanding dawned, and a slow smile spread across the big angel's face. In a deep, gentle voice, Lucan said, "Ah."

20
MUCH TO LEARN

Raz propped his fists on his hips and laughed aloud. "Only a Guardian could say so much without actually *saying* anything!"

The big angel's smile only broadened, and his gaze swung to Ethan. "Welcome. I am Lucan, apprentice to Othniel. God has placed Naomi Pomeroy under my watch-care, and my joy is full."

"I am Ethan, and this is Conrad." Glancing from face to face, he shyly asked, "When do I get to meet my charge?"

"Ah," replied Lucan, all understanding and sympathy.

"Take hold of patience, Guardian," Conrad said kindly. "You'll need the next nine months to prepare yourself."

UP WITH THE CHICKENS

Ethan was on the edge of his seat already, but he nearly jumped out of his chair when a sudden *thud* sounded overhead. Lucan's gaze drifted to the ceiling. "That would be Neil. He has the top bunk."

A few minutes later, a woman with sleepy gray eyes and a messy blonde braid shuffled into the kitchen, tightening the tie on her bathrobe. She yawned as she measured oatmeal and pulled juice glasses from the cupboard.

Conrad asked, "Naomi?"

"Yes," her guardian confirmed with a smile for Ethan. "The new life she carries is the one you will watch over."

22
Young Ones Underfoot

Ethan watched in awe as Naomi tended to her young family, reminding Tad to wear a hat while he took care of his chores, helping Neil locate a missing library book, neatly braiding Prissie's hair, and peeling a banana for Beau.

"Where are all their Guardians?" Ethan asked curiously.

"Close," Lucan replied. "You will grow used to Trumble's rotation."

"Trumble?" asked Conrad.

"The senior ranking Guardian in this Hedge," Raz supplied.

"As junior member, your place is here … inside," Lucan explained. "Of course, there will be times when Naomi leaves. Then, you are with me. We will guard her together."

23 Facing the Meantime

"So I must wait," Ethan murmured, already feeling restless. He'd never given Time much thought while in heaven, but already it weighed heavily on his mind.

"Even as she will wait," confirmed Lucan, nodding toward the mother-to-be.

"Your training will continue," said Conrad. "We will sharpen your blade and your skills."

"I am grateful for your guidance." Ethan smiled tentatively. "Will I be ready in time?"

Conrad's smirk returned. "You'll *never* feel ready, and yet your time will come."

"Facing the enemy is one thing," Lucan said. "Guarding a life is another."

"Why?"

Lucan shrugged. "People have such … individuality."

24
GRUFF ENCOURAGEMENT

Throughout the morning, Raz introduced Ethan to other members of the Pomeroy family's Hedge, ending with Lucan's mentor Othniel.

Bushy sideburns stood out like a russet mane on either side of the burly angel's broad face. His voice was a gravely growl as he asked, "Is it just me, or are Guardians getting younger?"

Ethan certainly *felt* young. Othniel towered head and shoulders above Conrad, whose height Ethan had yet to match. "I have much to learn," he offered humbly.

For all his gruffness, there was a kind light in Othniel's gray eyes as he said, "God is always wise."

Raz disappeared for a time and returned with two archers and five small boxes. "Lunch!" he cheerfully announced.

"Come aside and refresh yourself," urged Garrick.

Yannis said, "We'll keep you company!"

Ethan watched in frank fascination as the nearly-identical angels opened their lunches in perfect synchronization and inspected the contents.

Yannis elbowed his mentor, "Trade you?"

As they swapped, Ethan's mystification grew. "Are they not the same?"

"He still can't tell us apart!" whispered Yannis.

Garrick shrugged. "Give him time."

Ethan awkwardly fumbled for an explanation.

Raz laughed. "You walked right into that one."

"Oh. A joke?"

The archers dimpled.

26
DADDY'S HOME

Not long after the Pomeroy children returned from school, they sent up a shout. "Daddy's home! Daddy's home!"

While the kids mobbed their father, his slim Guardian approached Ethan. "Welcome!" he greeted in a light voice. "I'm Jomei, apprentice to Trumble. God has placed Jayce Pomeroy under my watch-care, and my joy is full."

Long, yellow hair and brilliant green wings reminded Ethan of daffodils. "I am Ethan."

Slanted eyes held a smile as Jomei added, "I suspect your charge will be *quite* the handful!"

"Why?"

"It's merely a guess, but you're like me," the Guardian explained. "Built for speed."

27
THE FAITHFUL

Ethan tipped his head one way and then the other. No matter how he studied Naomi Pomeroy, he couldn't tell that she was expecting a child. Even *she* wasn't yet aware of the life she carried. The only ones who knew were members of the Hedge, and only because Ethan had been Sent into their midst.

There was no evidence for his hope. This was the first time Ethan had been asked to trust in something unseen. "An angel must have faith as well?" he mused aloud.

Conrad glanced up from polishing his sword. "Have it and live by it."

28
Boot Laces

Biting his lip in concentration, Ethan undid his laces back down to the ankle. He was pretty sure he'd gone *over* when he should have gone *around* … maybe? Muttering under his breath, he talked himself through the complex pattern, this time getting it right.

Conrad glanced his way but didn't say anything.

Ethan sighed over still making such simple mistakes, but he had plenty of time for the practice he needed. "When I am not training, I wait; when I *am* training, I am still waiting."

"Complaining?"

"Merely restless."

"Merely *eager*," Conrad countered.

Ethan smiled, for his mentor was right.

Banding Together

They usually came at night, slipping like shadows, creeping like thieves. Their faces twisted with malice, and their wings creaking with empty ambitions. Ethan gripped his sword tightly, unnerved by the hissing lies and gnashing teeth, but then a bright arrow zinged through the darkness, scattering the Fallen.

"Your Flight is swift," Lucan remarked, his silver eyes trained skyward.

Ethan followed his gaze and spotted a flash of turquoise. He was glad that God had Sent Tycho to support them in their time of need. The young Guardian smiled grimly, then faced their foe, resolved to stand, ready to defend.

30
Angel Lullabies

Ethan liked Jomei's mentor Trumble. The silver-haired angel was an acrobatic fighter, nimbly wielding a long staff with crescent-shaped blades on either end. Trumble was neither the tallest nor broadest of the warriors defending the Pomeroys, but he was quite possibly the gentlest.

Late one night, Ethan caught a whisper of song, and he followed it to the bedroom where the boys slept. Trumble crouched at the end of one of the bunks, wings widespread as he hummed a soft tune. "Sing with me?" he invited.

Ethan gladly added the harmony.

Together, they drove away one little boy's bad dreams.

A FLUTTER OF LIFE

Eventually, Naomi realized that she was pregnant. Whispers about an addition to the family were followed by an announcement to the children about a new brother or sister. Jayce fussed, Naomi grumbled, Jomei laughed, and Lucan hovered. Ethan cast shy glances at the gentle swell of the woman's growing belly, his wings trembling in anticipation.

His favorite moments by far were the frequent prayers the Pomeroy family offered for the little one they were eager to meet, for they echoed his own yearnings. Ethan's songs grew sweeter as he thanked God for the love that stirred in his hopeful heart.

32
DAY OF RECKONING

That winter, two of the Pomeroy children put the entire Hedge on edge. Ethan had never seen such distraction. Even Conrad wasn't as focused as usual. Finally, Ethan took Trumble aside. "What is happening?"

"Can you feel it?"

"Yes, but I do not understand."

"You will," the silver-haired angel assured, leading him into the family room.

Jayce and Naomi were speaking seriously with Prissie and Beau, but they didn't seem to be scolding. Ethan stole closer. No one minded. In a matter of moments, the young Guardian grasped the direction this conversation was going. "These children," he gasped. "They *believe*!"

ROUGH AND TUMBLE

Heaven Rejoices

The children's prayers were simple, but heaven's response was profound. From every direction, Flights of angels came winging. Practically speaking, they lent support to a Hedge far too overcome by joy to be any use to their charges, but they weren't all warriors. Messengers darted in, loudly proclaiming the good news.

Ethan slipped outside to watch the skies fill and was nearly bowled over by the two Messengers from his own Flight. Raz was a frequent visitor to the Pomeroy farm, but his mentor always seemed to be busy elsewhere. Ethan got over his astonishment enough to exclaim, "Welcome, Verrill!"

34
You Are Here

Raz's mentor was tall and slender. Brown wings rustled into neat folds. Brown hands cradled a lap harp. Brown eyes warmed at Ethan's welcome. "I knew you'd be here!"

"Yes. This will be my charge's home."

"Will be?"

"The child has yet to be born," Ethan explained.

"All in good time," Verrill said, poking absently at the stray tendrils of green hair escaping from an intricate topknot. "But I meant that you're *here* because this is where I'm Sent."

"Sent?" Ethan glanced at Raz, who smiled fondly at his mentor and shrugged.

Verrill's brows arched. "With a message."

"For …?"

"*You.*"

35
SECONDHAND

It's said that each angelic order reflects some facet of their Creator. The malakim are heaven's Messengers, and their voices are likened to the voice of God, able to reach into the hearts and minds of the Faithful.

"You did not have to come here to tell me something," said Ethan.

Verrill laughed lightly. "You've never received a message from on high?"

"No." Shuffling his feet, the young Guardian said, "I do not understand. I have always heeded God's words."

Raz asked, "Can the Faithful do any less?"

"I'm not bringing a reprimand, Ethan," Verrill gently assured. "Only a warning."

36
CUT IT OUT

The Messenger's words riveted Ethan, so much so that the tumult of joy surrounding the farm faded from notice.

Holding the young Guardian's gaze, Verrill said, "There's a blight amidst the trees. If it isn't cut out, it will bear the fruit of destruction."

Ethan puzzled over the message. Diseased trees sounded more like a Caretaker's problem. Why would God warn someone like *him* about a blight? Ethan snapped to attention. "Is something in the orchard?"

"Sure sounds that way," Raz said, gazing toward acres of trees.

"Then we should find it!"

"*You*," corrected Verrill. "This task is yours, Ethan."

WHERE THREE ARE GATHERED

"Alone?" Ethan asked in disbelief. "But this danger concerns the whole Hedge!"

Verrill's gaze took on a far-off quality, and he plucked idly at his harp's strings. "You won't be entirely alone. Raz and I bear witness to the message. Confer with us at any time."

Raz nodded several times. "We're here for you."

Ethan accepted this with a small smile. "Does any direction accompany the warning?"

With a hand across the strings, Verrill silenced his instrument. "Think before you speak. Don't lose sight of what's true. Lay bare the lies, exposing their root. Only then can it be severed."

38
THE LAY OF THE LAND

Ethan wasn't sure how to go about being secretive, so he didn't even try. "I want to walk the orchard."

His teammates exchanged looks, but Trumble smiled. "An excellent way to learn the terrain … and to fend off the restlessness that comes with waiting. I will join you."

In succeeding weeks, each time Trumble's rotation gave the young Guardian a break from the house, they walked together—up one row, down the next. Winter became spring, and the orchard bloomed. Spring became summer, and green apples slowly bent gnarled branches.

Ethan remained alert, but he saw no signs of blight.

39

SATURDAY MORNING

"The first eight months go by fine, but the ninth feels like an eternity," Naomi complained to her mother-in-law.

Nell Pomeroy chuckled as she flipped pancakes. "This too shall pass. Something you know better than most."

Ethan shuffled his feet, too fidgety to join Lucan at the table. *Soon!* His whole being vibrated with anticipation. From the pensive expression on Lucan's face, *he* sensed it, too.

Just then, a familiar voice echoed through Ethan's mind. *'Are you restless, child of light?'*

"No more than this good woman," he murmured.

'Her travail begins.'

Naomi gasped. Nell turned. Lucan stood. Ethan sat.

40
TRAVAIL

Conrad helped Ethan off the floor. "On your feet, Guardian. Your time has come!"

When Jayce rushed home to take his wife to the hospital, Trumble literally picked Ethan up, carrying him in his arms as they followed. He tried to protest, but the silver-haired angel murmured, "Hush. You are shaking so hard, your wings would crumple." Seeing the young apprentice's embarrassment, Trumble added, "It was the same for us all."

"It's true," assured Conrad, who flew with sword in hand.

Unable to do anything more, Ethan fixed his eyes on the angel-flanked mini-van and trusted the rest to God.

LIFELONG COMPANION

Prayers kept Guardians close, and Jayce's came in a steady stream, interspersed with words of reassurance for his wife. Jomei knelt at the man's side, offering the shelter of his wings, and Lucan's large hand rested close to Naomi's clenched fist.

Ethan could see the gentle expression in his silver eyes, and his breath hitched as the enormity of his task weighed upon him. This child's whole lifetime lay before him, and the prospect was overwhelming.

"One day at a time, Ethan," Conrad quietly urged, wrapping an arm around his shoulders. "You only need courage for the day you're in."

42
SANCTUARY

Since Naomi's doctor and both of the nurses bustling around the maternity suite were believers, angels flanked the entire room by the time birth was imminent. Ethan hardly knew how to meet so many sympathetic gazes, but their support buoyed him.

More than anything, he felt as if the room had become a sanctuary, and he was unable to remain silent when God was so near. Ethan's soft hum was immediately joined by Trumble's. One by one, the others added to the song.

Met by joy, heralded by angels, loved by God, Ethan's charge took his first breath … and wailed.

Visiting Hours

Mere minutes after the baby's birth, Tycho strode into the crowded room.

Ethan straightened in surprise at seeing his captain and stammered out a greeting. "Were you Sent?"

"No." Tycho shook his head bemusedly. "Does it seem strange to you that I would come?"

"I do not know," Ethan confessed. "This is the first time I have been part of a Flight."

The tall Protector smiled faintly and nodded toward the newborn. "This child is under your watch-care."

"Yes."

"Just as *you* are under *mine*."

Ethan blinked, then gravely replied, "Now, I see."

Tycho nodded. "Yes, I thought you might."

44
An Angel's Tears

Ethan had trained for this day, and he knew his duty well. Drawing his sword, he put his tiny charge at his back, fully prepared to defend him with all he had. His joy overflowed … to such a degree that he kept having to drag the back of his hand across his eyes.

Conrad strolled over. "Your stance is good, but there'll be time enough for you to hold this position. For now, why don't you get to know your new counterpart?"

"Is that allowed?" Ethan asked.

"It is *encouraged*," Conrad assured. "Watch him, and I'll watch over you both."

 Rough and Tumble

Visiting hours ended. The lights dimmed. As soon as the door clicked shut, Naomi eased out of bed and shuffled over to collect her baby from his crib. Nestling down beside him on the single bed, she gazed at her son in the half-light, gently stroking the fuzz of blond hair atop his head. "I'm so glad you're here," she murmured.

Ethan, who knelt as close to the bed as he dared, blinked in surprise.

Laughing softly, Naomi amended, "Well, I guess you've always been *close*, haven't you?"

The young guardian knew she couldn't see him, but he nodded anyhow.

46
Under His Hand

Raz arrived in the hospital room with a swirl of lime green light. "I hear you have glad tidings of great joy! Are you as happy as you look?"

"I am."

Lifting his wings clear, the Messenger folded his angular frame into a bedside chair. "You're *also* looking a little faded around the edges. Time to eat!" As manna spread sweetness over Ethan's tongue, Raz cleared his throat. "So can I see your sword?"

With a bashful sort of pride, Ethan watched his friend trace the letters that had appeared on its hilt.

"It's a good name."

Ethan nodded. "Hezekiah."

WATCHFUL ONE

A bassinet had been crowded into the corner of Jayce and Naomi's bedroom, and Ethan's favorite perch was the tufted footstool in front of her rocking chair. The sheathed sword on his back didn't scrape the floor, and there was room to unfurl his wings. Ethan could sit with his knees pulled up to his chest, watching over his sleeping charge.

The baby's face scrunched up, and after a toothless yawn, blue eyes blinked open.

Ethan brightened, and he gently wafted pink wings.

With a burble of excitement, one tiny hand reached toward the bright mobile that twirled beguilingly overhead.

48
RESPITE

"Go. You need this."

At Conrad's urging, Ethan accepted Yannis and Garrick's offer to accompany him outside the Hedge. Trusting his charge to his mentor's watch-care, Ethan chased the two cherubim as they spiraled through pelting rain, heedless of the storm, but watchful of their surroundings.

Trusting their protection, Ethan relaxed his guard and reveled in the feel of wind under his wings. Beating upwards, he burst through iron gray clouds into blazing sunlight. Flight became a dance of worship as the angels whirled higher.

When Ethan finally turned homeward, he felt lighter despite the weight of his new responsibilities.

49

MEEK AND MIGHTY

Babies rarely strayed far from their mothers, so Ethan and Lucan were as close as ever. The pair trailed after Naomi, who was strolling through the orchard's wide rows when a clatter rang out nearby. Lucan darted into the air to assess the situation, and when the big angel's boots hit the ground, he drew twin swords. Silver eyes ablaze, he announced, "Othniel and Conrad are beset. Stand ready."

With a curt nod, Ethan unsheathed his weapon. Guardians might be meek, but no one could discount their fierceness when it came to fulfilling their duty to God. "I am ready."

50
SHORT AND SWEET

Ethan loitered on the edge of the family room, watching Jayce Pomeroy make the most ridiculous faces at his youngest son. The little guy had learned to smile, and his proud papa was helping him show off the newfound ability. According to Trumble's rotation, it was time for Ethan to move outdoors, leaving Lucan and Jomei on guard inside the house, yet he lingered.

Jomei wandered over, warning, "You're going to be late again. Rest easy. Hezekiah is safe."

"They began calling him Zeke today."

"I wondered if they'd shorten his name. It's … cute."

Ethan couldn't have agreed more.

Little Ears, Little Eyes

The children were back in school, leaving Naomi home with her youngest. Since she kept Zeke close, Ethan trailed after both of them, watching with frank curiosity as she included her baby in one-sided conversations or sang along with the radio to him. News and nonsense. Plans and prayers. Zeke tracked the sound of her voice, wide eyes following her with infantile adoration.

Ethan wasn't much different. For now, he was getting to know Naomi more than Zeke, but he didn't mind. Mothers shaped their children, and she was doing so now, artlessly pouring her love into his young charge.

52
CARRY ON

Othniel jerked Ethan from his reverie. "Do apples offend you? Or is it the trees that bear them?"

"What? No!"

The big warrior scratched thoughtfully at one of his bristling sideburns as he scanned the moonlit orchard. "You look as if you expect them to attack."

Ethan cautiously replied, "Something could be hiding amidst them."

"Unlikely." Othniel's wings spread wide as he prepared to move on. "But your vigilance is appreciated."

The gruff old guardian rarely offered compliments, but Ethan only managed a scant smile. He knew better, and that made him feel wretched. Where could their foe be hiding?

What's Needed

Ethan watched Naomi aim spoonfuls of pureed carrot. If Zeke had simply let her feed him, the meal could have met a tidy end. But he didn't. And it hadn't. Orange dribbled down his chin, smeared across his nose, and made his hair stand on end.

"*Ethan*," called Conrad.

"Sorry. What were you saying?"

"Only that you should pay close attention," his mentor repeated dryly. "To see what he needs."

He propped his chin on both fists. "A bath?"

"A firm hand. A close watch." As Naomi giggled and reached for her camera, Conrad smirked. "And a sense of humor."

54
HARVESTTIME

When Ethan had arrived the previous autumn, harvest was nearing its end. It was hard to believe something like selling apples could lead to such an inundation of color and chaos. "Is it always like this?"

"Every year." Raz grinned. "Must be half a legion overhead!"

"At least it is quiet here." The two of them sat on the floor behind the counter, guarding Zeke's carrier.

"Don't be so sure," the Messenger warned. "Babies have a way of drawing crowds."

Ethan nodded. He'd seen it often enough at church.

As if on cue, an old woman crowed, "*There he is!*"

Bouncing Baby Boy

A perfect stranger scooped up Ethan's charge, jostling the baby from his sleep. The Guardian was on his feet. He glanced urgently toward Naomi, who was busy at the cash register. Did she realize Zeke had been baby-napped?

Raz laughed. "Relax, Ethan. He's in no danger."

A gaggle of women soon crowded around, and the boy bounced from one pair of arms to the next.

"Such a charmer!"

"What a darling!"

The Guardian was finally beginning to relax when one of them exclaimed, "I think I'll take him home!"

Ethan's expression of utter dismay sent Raz into gales of laughter.

56
HAND TO MOUTH

L ucan and Ethan sat side-by-side at the big kitchen table waiting for sunrise. "I would stay close to young Zeke," the silver-eyed angel advised.

"Why?"

"At this age, everything a little one gets his hands onto ends up in his mouth." Lucan's slow smile made an appearance. "You *may* need to discretely intervene."

Sure enough, at breakfast, Zeke spied a stray apple core left on the table. When he stretched to reach it from his highchair, Ethan hastily bumped it onto the floor. Hopefully, Neil wouldn't get in *too* much trouble later when his mother found it under the table.

ROUGH AND TUMBLE

CAUGHT UP

Yannis looped an arm around Ethan's shoulders. "You've been avoiding us."

"I saw you yesterday."

"One day can be like a thousand years!"

Ethan protested, "I was about to join you."

"Your wings are still furled," pointed out Garrick. "Good thing Conrad sent us to pry you away."

Yannis chivvied him outside. "Tycho is holding up evensong."

"I am late?"

"Catches on quick," whispered mentor to apprentice.

They were higher than the trees before Ethan could even begin to spread his wings. A lone Guardian on the barn roof lifted his hand in salute as the cherubim carried him off.

58
UNISON

They arrived in his Flight's tent, and Ethan shuffled over to Tycho. "I am late."

"Yet most welcome," his captain assured.

Yannis and Garrick dragged him to where Conrad waited, and once they sat, Verrill struck a chord on his harp.

Ethan *loved* evensong.

He had seemingly little in common with these rugged archers, but as they spun their day's events into songs of praise, surprising patterns emerged. Lessons overlapped. Purposes blended. It didn't take an Observer to see God's hand at work.

They were teammates, sharing a deep trust. They were the Faithful, serving the One who embodies faithfulness.

MOBILITY

Jomei called Ethan over. "Your boy's learned a new trick."

"I already know he can fit his foot in his mouth," Ethan said, glancing toward the far end of the room where the older Pomeroy siblings knelt in a row.

The kids thumped their hands on the floor. "This way, Zeke! Do it again!"

"What is it they expect him … to …."

Ethan trailed off as the answer became obvious. Zeke couldn't creep or crawl yet, but he could roll. Over and over. Right across the room.

As his family applauded his accomplishment, Jomei laughed. "On your toes, Guardian. He's mobile."

Mother Knows Best

Ethan willingly faced terrible foes, but Zeke's tears were his undoing. What could be wrong? Why wasn't Naomi rushing to her baby's side?

Eventually, the woman strolled through the door, calmly picked up her son, tested his diaper, held him close, and firmly said, "Diaper's dry. Tummy's full. Bedtime's here. May as well give up, little man. Your momma's wise to your tricks." With that, she tucked him in.

Zeke wailed, but Naomi didn't return.

To Ethan's surprise, the boy's head popped up, his chin quivered, then he slowly lay back down, blinked several times, and drifted off to sleep.

Thanksgiving

Ethan smiled bemusedly at his charge's antics during dinner. Zeke babbled non-stop, grabbed the glasses off his maternal grandmother's face, and gummed a potato roll while kicking the table. His personality was steadily emerging, and Ethan found each detail fascinating. The way Zeke's hair curled against his neck. The way his nose wrinkled whenever he laughed. The way his eyebrows arched if something caught his interest.

Every other Guardian found a reason to slip into the house during the Thanksgiving feast. It was the same for each one—eager to understand, longing to serve, grateful to have found such love.

62
TUNE YOUR EARS

Ethan was so absorbed in watching Grandma Nell offering spoonfuls of mashed potatoes to Zeke, he didn't notice Raz's intentions until the Messenger pushed a pinch of manna into his mouth.

"If you prefer, I can find a spoon!" teased his teammate.

Snatching away the box of food, Ethan mumbled, "I will manage. Thank you."

Green eyes grew serious. "So how's the search going?"

"Not well. I am not sure where else to look."

"Are you supposed to look … or listen?" Raz explained, "Whispers of doubts, seeds of dissent, harmful half-truths—these, too, are attacks and can lead to destruction."

 ROUGH AND TUMBLE

ICE STORM

After the storm, sunlight glittered harshly against trees glazed by ice. Brittle branches bowed and broke, causing an eerie racket throughout the Pomeroys' acreage. Ethan whispered, "Beautiful, but also terrible."

Conrad nodded. "I wonder if a Caretaker will be Sent to salvage the trees."

They found Trumble behind the barns, kneeling beside a ruined beehive. Wax and comb, queen and drone were scattered and spoiled.

"Trouble?" Conrad asked sharply.

"Perhaps."

Ethan didn't understand. "Why?"

"The Fallen—especially the newly Fallen—have been known to ravage hives," Trumble explained. "They remember the sweetness of manna and can no longer get it."

64

TRACKS IN THE SNOW

"**D**o you suspect the enemy?" Conrad drew his sword and scanned the trees lining the nearby pond.

Trumble gestured to the ice-glazed snow. "These tracks suggest otherwise, but I'll follow them to be sure."

Was *this* the danger? Ethan quickly asked, "May I join you?"

"Certainly."

Conrad took their leader's post, allowing Trumble and Ethan to investigate. Tracks led into an older section of the orchard where unremarkable trees stretched endlessly in every direction. But the scanty trail didn't end in front of a burrow or den. Amidst branches bent nearly to the ground, the Guardians found snow stained scarlet.

TRACES OF DEATH

"Blood."

"Death." Trumble picked up one of the pheasant feathers scattered on the snow-covered ground. "Fox, I think. Pete won't be pleased to learn there's a predator this close to his ducks."

"Are you certain? Did *you* see a den when we walked the acreage?"

"No. But I wasn't looking for hidey-holes."

"I was," the younger angel said solemnly. "No dens. No burrows."

"Pete fills in those he finds to discourage resettlement." Trumble rose and looked toward the park lands to the east. "A fox is the likeliest explanation."

Ethan nodded. "May I keep searching?"

Trumble smiled. "Until you're satisfied."

66
NEWFALLEN

The next day, they found another broken and battered hive. Grandpa Pete built a fence, and Trumble repositioned the guard. Sitting beside Othniel atop the house, Ethan stared up into the gentle drift of new snow and quietly asked, "How do angels Fall?"

"By choice," the big warrior replied.

"But … why?"

"You cannot imagine such a thing?"

Ethan slowly shook his head. "No."

"Just as well you cannot."

"But … the hives," the younger Guardian pressed. "If the enemy is to blame, doesn't that mean that the Fallen one regrets his choice?"

Gazing skyward, Othniel said, "They all do."

JOIN THE TRIUMPH
OF THE SKIES

The Hedge's daily pattern changed in December. Naomi made several trips into neighboring towns, and a sense of anticipation built whenever she squirreled away packages. As Lucan followed her lead, he remarked, "Christmas is near."

Hearts were light. Songs were shared. But some of them made Ethan uneasy. "They sing of angels. Would it not be better to sing of God?"

"We are mentioned because we are part of the story," Lucan said. "These hymns are passed down, and each generation joins the chorus. Fellow servants, now fellow heralds."

After that, Ethan found himself humming along with the prolonged glorias.

68
CHOSEN ONE

Ethan happened to be there when Naomi's mother-in-law bustled into the kitchen.

"I have big news!"

"Did something come up during the Christmas committee meeting?"

Nell Pomeroy beamed. "It's all decided. Our Zeke will be in the manger this year!"

"Really?" Naomi gasped.

"Well, he's the only one who's not too big, nor too small. It was plain sense to give him the part!"

Naomi crossed to the playpen and swooped up her baby, cuddling him close. "We'd be *delighted* to include this young man in the living nativity!"

From that night on, "Away in a Manger" became Zeke's lullaby.

69 THE PRETTIEST ANGEL

Five apprentice Guardians crowded into Grandma Nell's sewing room during their charges' final fittings. Tad and Neil were shepherds, and Prissie and Beau were angels.

Ethan endured friendly jostling as Naomi tried to soothe her five-year-old daughter's ruffled feathers. "But sweetheart, everyone else will have gold halos."

"But pink's *prettier*." Prissie pouted. "God *needs* pink angels!"

Tad's Guardian laughed outright, and Beau's rumbled, "Amen and amen!"

As the others made room, Ethan spread rosy wings over Prissie and quietly declared, "Pink and gold, orange and blue—we are merely the rainbow wreathing God's throne. *His* beauty will capture your heart."

70
LIVELY NATIVITY

It didn't take long for Zeke to kick free of his swaddling clothes. Wriggling and twisting, he peered inquisitively at everything from the Christmas lights overhead to the sheep pen next to the living nativity's stable. In the first twenty minutes of his role as newborn Savior, Zeke untied Joseph's robe and yanked Mary's veil askew. Ethan watched in amazement as his charge next discovered he could crawl. Straight up.

With remarkable calm, Jayce stepped in, plucking his teetering son from Mary's shoulder and giving him an expert toss.

Cameras flashed on every side as baby Jesus squealed with laughter.

FATHER'S FOOTSTEPS

Christmas afternoon, Jayce fell asleep on the floor in front of the tree. Ethan was certain he'd intended to provide a barrier; instead, he became Zeke's step-stool.

"This brings back memories," Jomei remarked, casually jostling a bell-laden branch.

To Ethan's relief, Jayce woke in time to prevent catastrophe.

Tapping Zeke's nose, Jayce lectured, "Now, son, don't get ahead of yourself. I still have a scar from the first time I pulled down the tree. I was three. You have *plenty* of time to make your mark!"

A smile quirked Ethan's lips. "He was the same?"

Jomei chuckled. "Very much so."

72
Direct Intervention

Every time Zeke reached for his new ball, it rolled away. He scooted after, but only managed to bump his toy closer to the top of the back stairway.

"No, no," his Guardian whispered, to no avail.

Zeke teetered.

Ethan dove.

Hooking a finger into the baby's diaper, he kept Zeke from the edge, but the boy struggled, babbling at the ball that bounced away.

Naomi leaned out the door where she'd been making beds. "Good gracious!" she exclaimed, snatching him up. "You're *not* supposed to wander off like this. Come keep me company, little man."

Zeke giggled.

Ethan sagged.

Ethan sat at the top of the stairs, dazed. Although he'd kept Zeke safe, his heart still raced. And though he didn't know what the future might hold, he felt certain the dangers would multiply with the years. Was this a Guardian's lot?

With a rush of wings, Conrad appeared at the bottom of the stairs. Catching sight of his apprentice's face, his dark eyes widened in surprise … then softened with sympathy. He hurried to kneel before the younger angel and offered his hand. "Why am I Sent to you?"

Ethan took a shaky breath. "Because I am afraid."

74
GROWING PAINS

"What happened?" Conrad asked.

Ethan gestured at the ball that had rolled to a stop at the base of the stairs. "Zeke nearly fell. I held him back."

His mentor nodded. "And?"

"I did not realize how much he *needs* me."

"Is that what you think?"

Hunching his shoulders, Ethan asked, "Am I wrong?"

"You're half-right." Tapping Ethan's breastplate, Conrad said, "There's *you* to consider."

"Me?"

"In His wisdom, God put the two of you together." The wiry warrior smirked. "Being Zeke's guardian has already changed you more than all your years as my apprentice."

"I have changed?"

"You've *grown*."

One of the Boys

"Are you sure you want to bring Zeke?" Naomi asked, rummaging through a basket of knit hats.

"Sure, sure." Jayce tossed a striped scarf at Neil before kneeling to tie Beau's boots. "He's old enough to be included in manly expeditions."

Naomi fit red fleece mittens onto Zeke, then rummaged in the coat closet. "I *know* I saved Beau's old snowsuit."

Ethan barely listened to these plans. He was much more interested in Zeke's somber concentration. The little guy sat in his carrier seat, slowly opening and closing his hands, apparently trying to figure out why his fingers were missing.

76
AFTERNOON RAMBLE

Snowshoe treks through the orchard were Jayce's prescription for restless Sunday afternoons.

Ethan and Jomei fell in step behind the man and his four sons while Trumble kept watch from high above. As the children jostled noisily for their father's attention, Jomei casually inquired, "Ever wonder why we don't leave any footprints?"

"No." Ethan glanced down at the odd tracks the Pomeroys were leaving behind, then peered over his shoulder. Even though he could feel the crunch of snow under his feet, their boots left no traces.

"Are you wondering now?"

"...Yes."

"Footprints!" Tad exclaimed, causing both Guardians to startle.

Hunting We Will Go

With a quick wingbeat, Ethan landed in front of the Pomeroys. Neil crouched before the tracks that angled across their path. "Betcha it's a *wolf*!"

Tad snickered. "Probably a barn cat."

Jayce leaned forward, causing the baby in the carrier on his back to squeal happily. "Actually, I think it's a coon."

"Here?" Tad asked, frowning.

"Raccoons like apples," Beau reported. "Maybe he was hungry."

Jayce shook his head. "Plenty of apples to be had without wandering *this* far into your grandpa's orchard."

"Can we follow 'em?" Neil wheedled.

"Sure, sure," their father replied amiably. "Let's hunt down our trespasser."

78
HEARING THINGS

Trumble dropped down to walk with Jomei while Ethan rushed ahead, anxious to confirm that their trespasser was nothing more than an animal. Sense insisted that it must be. Slowing to a standstill, he paused to consider. If angels left no sign of their passing, wouldn't it be the same for the Fallen?

Suddenly, the hint of a sound reached his ears. A hissing. A creaking. Wait … was that laughter?

Drawing his sword, Ethan slowly turned in a circle, trying to pinpoint its source.

"Spoil the fruit, spoils of war."

The sing-song grating sent a chill down the Guardian's spine.

Death Rattle

The boys' voices neared, so Ethan quickly retraced his steps. Sword in hand, he followed the tracks until they ended several rows over. Dirty snow. Clawed earth. Scattered stones. Mangled bark. Blood streaked the angry gashes, which meant that the creature who'd fought to hide amidst this apple tree's roots had injured itself.

"Come out," Ethan ordered.

A feeble growl. A rush of wind. A deathly silence.

Jayce took one look and borrowed Neil's scarf to mark the tree, then hurried the boys away, lecturing them on the dangers of approaching wounded animals.

Ethan knew better. The coon was dead.

80
STEADY STREAM

Ethan quietly asked, "Is he ill?"

Amusement flashed in Conrad's dark eyes. "What gives you that impression?"

The young Guardian couldn't quite tear his eyes away from the long strand of saliva trembling from Zeke's bottom lip. "There is an excess of …."

"Drool," his mentor finished. "I remember this part. He's teething."

As the boy blew spit bubbles, Ethan resisted the urge to reach out and wipe his chin. "So he is in no danger?"

"He'll experience some discomfort."

Zeke gnawed on a block, adding a slick of saliva to its brightly-colored surface.

Ethan wryly added, "And much dampness."

Make a Joyful Noise

On Sunday morning, the senior member of the Hedge surrounding First Baptist Church sought out Ethan. "Go inside. Your young charge is causing a stir."

Ethan quickly entered, scanning the sanctuary for Zeke. Several other Guardians flanked the room, including Lucan, who smiled broadly.

Then Ethan heard one voice clashing with the opening hymn's chords. Boisterous *la-la-la*s drew indulgent looks from those nearby. Even the worship director was grinning. And when the music stopped, Zeke enjoyed a prolonged solo.

As Naomi hustled her son out a side door, Ethan followed, humming a soft counterpoint to Zeke's exuberant song of praise.

82
Daddy's Boy

"They're inseparable."

"It was love at first sight," Naomi assured her friend. "For both of them."

Ethan followed her gaze across the church's fellowship hall, to where Jayce stood with Zeke cradled in the crook of his arm.

"It's good for boys to love their daddies. And Jayce is a pro."

"You'd *think* so." Naomi laughed at her husband's expression when he finally realized his young son was gumming his necktie. Extracting the wreckage of sodden silk from the boy's grip, Jayce contemplated it, shrugged, and gave it back.

Shaking her head, Naomi confessed, "Zeke's made rookies of us both."

83
SLEEP SWEET

"Whaddya say we sack out down here?" Jayce mumbled huskily as he carried his fussing son to the couch. He murmured encouragement and prayers while Zeke clung and cried, and Ethan extended his wings over them until they dozed. When Zeke began to squirm again, Ethan gingerly picked up where Jayce left off, massaging the baby's tender gums.

The Guardian's heart lurched when Zeke grabbed onto his finger, holding tightly while he blinked up at his angel. Caught off guard, Ethan blinked back.

Gradually, Zeke's eyes drifted shut.

On this night, sleep was a miracle that tasted faintly of manna.

84
January Thaw

The following day brought a thaw. Clear skies. Warm sun. Soft breezes. Snowdrifts sank into slush, and birds made a cheerful racket at the feeders. The Pomeroy women conspired to open windows and air bedding.

Ethan shared the clothesline post with a whole row of chickadees while watching over Zeke, who sat in a blanket-filled basket next to his grandmother.

Zeke rocked determinedly back and forth, toppling the laundry basket and gaining his prize—a handful of snow.

Grandma Nell rescued and righted the boy, and Ethan chuckled as his little mister grinned, showing off two sharp, little, white teeth.

85
TEAMWORK

"Oop, oop, oop!" Ethan murmured, hooking a finger into Zeke's overalls to prevent him from crawling over the back of his high chair and onto a neighboring sideboard. To the Guardian's chagrin, Zeke used him as a counterbalance.

In a stretch that defied gravity, the boy's fingers brushed a blue vase with its arrangement of pussy-willows.

Ethan tugged. Zeke grabbed.

Water sloshed. Glass shattered.

Lucan saw. Ethan winced. "Oops."

The big warrior shook his head bemusedly. "You are by his side, but *on* his side?"

Naomi rushed into the room right as her son cheerfully said his first word. "Uh-oh!"

86
STAND IN THE GAP

Grandpa Pete took to calling Zeke a little Houdini. Buckles, straps, ties, snaps, laces, and latches—he was their undoing. About the same time the youngster began pulling himself up and cruising, Zeke earned the reputation as both escape artist … and streaker. He'd conquered the baby gate, but an unseen angel barred the way.

"Patience, little mister," Ethan urged.

Inexplicably stranded, Zeke sat on the rug and pulled off his socks before tangling with the buttons of his overalls. He was down to a diaper by the time his siblings chorused, "Daddy's home!"

The Guardian retreated. Reinforcements had arrived.

87

BABY'S FIRST HAIRCUT

The orchard was in full bloom the day Grandpa Pete gave up. "That only made it worse."

Jayce sighed. "Options?"

"You've got two," his father announced. "Tell Naomi *now*... or *after* we get back from the barber."

Tossing Zeke over his shoulder, Jayce said, "Let's go."

Ethan trailed behind the men as they snuck from the machine shed to the car. He winged after them as they drove into town.

The Pomeroys' barber took one look at Zeke and asked, "Do I even *want* to know?"

Jayce groaned. "*Long* story … involving a litter of kittens, a caulking gun, and pruning shears."

88
FUTURE FARMER

The Pomeroys' sandbox was an old tractor tire set under a tree in their back yard, but Zeke wandered away from it, in search of his own fun. Ethan followed him to the garden, crouching when the boy thumped to sit in soft dirt.

"Sand would have brushed off," Ethan said conversationally.

Zeke patted the soil, squeezed a handful, then tasted the stuff.

"And you are flattening seedlings."

Tad found his little brother, and serious gray eyes took on a shine. "Putting down roots, Zeke?" Raking his fingers through the soil, he proudly said, "That's good. 'Cause this is home."

89
UMBRELLA STROLLER

While the older children explored Sunderland State Park's nature center, Jayce entertained Zeke with a stroller ride. Ethan jerked to attention when the man yelped, "Whoa!"

Zeke giggled and repeated his new trick, flinging his arms forward. It looked as if he'd pitch right out of the stroller, but Jayce double-checked the buckle. "Guess there's no harm in adding a little excitement to the ride."

They startled several passersby.

One elderly gentleman gleefully remarked, "Thinks he's Superman!"

His wife chortled. "Quite the daredevil!"

Jayce laughed and walked on, but Ethan gazed after the couple with a stunned expression. "God forbid."

90
PROVOCATION

Ethan sought out his mentor and blurted, "Zeke is no devil!"

Conrad's eyebrows slowly lifted at his apprentice's indignant explanation. Finally, he said, "Fly with me."

Vibrant wings carried them skyward.

Veer. Plunge. Dart. Spin. Conrad cut so close to Ethan that the young Guardian faltered, flustered and frustrated.

Drawing his sword, Conrad invited, "Defend him!"

Rush. Swing. Crash. Slam. Ethan fought to exhaustion's edge, eyes wet with unshed tears.

"Now tell me what they couldn't hear."

White knuckles throttling the hilt that bore his charge's name, Ethan sobbed, "He will *not* be like the Fallen!"

"May it be so."

"Look, Zeke!" Neil exclaimed. "We broughtcha blocks!"

"Don't fib," Prissie scolded.

"You'll like these," Tad coaxed. "Dad made 'em special."

Zeke stopped chewing off the point of his party hat and stared hard at his audience. Ethan smiled at the boy's expression when Jayce leaned in, snatching the topmost block and biting it in half.

"Not bad, if I do say so myself!" he said with a boyish grin.

Prissie giggled. "Daddy makes the *best* cakes!"

Quickly trading awe for messy enjoyment, Zeke ate while his family sang "Happy Birthday."

Ethan's and Conrad's own rendition lasted long into the night.

92
In Need of Rest

Raz found Ethan in the hayloft. "How d'ya feel?"

"Tired of this confinement." An enemy's poisoned dart had stolen his strength, searing his insides with lingering fire.

His friend pressed a cool hand to his forehead. "Healing takes time."

Ethan fidgeted miserably. "Did you happen to see Zeke?"

"He's tucked into his crib, sleeping off that fever," the Messenger reported. "Kinda like you."

"Conrad?"

"Right there," Raz assured, extending his wings over his teammate. "And I'm right here. And Tycho's on the roof. So rest."

Ethan relaxed enough to drift into dreams, which brought him closer to heaven and home.

THE NEW MAILMAN

"**D**id you hear about Milo? He's been made a Graft, just like his mentor!"

"No one needed to tell me. I saw him." Ethan stretched out a hand, fretfully searching for his sword. They'd taken it. And his armor. With a sigh, he explained, "I was Sent to his defense."

"Did he look strange?"

"He looked … like a mailman." Ethan admitted, "I did not recognize him at first."

"It's so exciting! Grafts are really rare!"

Ethan shifted restlessly on his makeshift bed. "Why has he taken on human guise?"

Raz shrugged. "Ask him yourself. Milo's joining us for evensong."

94
GRAFTED IN

Milo ambled over. "Hey, Ethan. I didn't get a chance to thank you earlier."

The young warrior demurred, "I was Sent."

"And I'm glad you were." Milo was well-known to everyone in the Hedge. He served in the same Flight as Prissie's Guardian. "I had an *eventful* first day on the job."

"Are Grafts often in danger?"

Milo nodded. "But *I* was Sent, and I couldn't be happier!"

"Why?"

"Oh, for lots of reasons. Not the least of which is coming up this Sunday." Turning to address those gathered, Milo announced, "The Pomeroys have invited me over for Sunday dinner!"

A Man on the Inside

J omei extended a hand. "Whether angel or human, you're a welcome guest, Milo."

Trumble chuckled. "You missed his point, Apprentice."

"A Messenger is always a messenger, no matter his trappings," Othniel said, scratching a bristling, red sideburn.

"And that presents an unusual opportunity," agreed Trumble.

The assembled Guardians traded glances, and Milo spread his arms wide. "In a few days, I'll talk to each of your charges. If there's anything you want them to know, I'd be happy to bear your messages. Subtly, of course."

Othniel's gravelly voice ended the stunned silence. "Compose yourselves. Compose your thoughts. Compose a message."

96
PRISSIE'S PRINCE

Ethan tested his wings, slowly circling the barn. Glimpsing a splash of orange, he drifted down to where Tamaes leaned against a tree near the roadside. Moments later, seven-year-old Prissie skipped along the driveway and climbed onto the white plank fence behind the mailboxes.

"Does she come here often?" Ethan asked curiously.

"She does now."

"Why?"

"Watch and see," Tamaes suggested.

Within minutes, the new mailman arrived. "Good afternoon, Miss Priscilla. Here again today?"

Ethan whispered, "She wished to see Milo?"

Tamaes nodded. "He is her prince."

As his bafflement increased, Ethan gave thanks that Zeke was not a girl.

ENTERTAINING ANGELS

Although a new Graft, Milo did well juggling the visible and invisible. When Grandma Nell slid more fried chicken onto his plate, he exclaimed, "Thank you, ma'am. Everything's delicious!"

Jayce passed potato rolls. "You fit right in around here."

"Nice and snug," Milo agreed with a laugh. With Neil crowding close on one side and Prissie on the other, he had to watch his elbows.

"You don't mind?" Naomi checked.

"Not a bit. Thanks for extending hospitality to someone like me."

"A newcomer?" Jayce asked.

"A neighbor," Naomi countered.

Milo said, "How about fellow servant."

Jayce grinned. "How about *friend*?"

KID FRIENDLY

M ilo sat in the middle of the family room floor and was quickly mobbed by children. He gave the Pomeroy youngsters his full attention, chatting amiably with each. Ethan was awed by how easily the Messenger wove each Guardian's message into his conversation, turning them into words of encouragement.

Tad's respect. Neil's discernment. Prissie's loyalty. Beau's faith.

"You're good with kids," Jayce remarked, joining their guest on the floor. He brought a freshly-scrubbed Zeke with him.

"I've always been a people person," the mailman replied. Ethan's breath caught when Milo held out his hands and asked, "Can I hold him?"

PRECIOUS IN HIS SIGHT

"Sure, sure. Zeke's not shy," Jayce replied, setting the little boy on his feet. "Go say *hi* to Mr. Leggett."

Without hesitation, Zeke toddled over to the newcomer, reached up, and grabbed the Messenger's nose. Milo … *honk*ed.

"'Onk!" echoed Zeke.

"Honk!" Milo agreed, scooping up the youngster and swinging him from side to side.

As his charge giggled, Ethan stole closer, amazed to think that his Zeke was safely cradled in the arms of an angel.

With a chuckle, the divine Messenger addressed Zeke in gentle tones. "Hey there, young sir. Do you have *any* idea how much you're loved?"

100
PEEK A BOO

Milo's voice was a whisper in Ethan's mind. *"Come closer, friend."*

Ethan eased up behind the other angel, peering over Milo's shoulder at Zeke. The Messenger hummed a few snatches of a melody the Guardian knew at once—the lullaby he often sang. With a grateful throb of his heart, Ethan joined in.

Midway through the duet, Zeke blinked.

When his focus shifted to Ethan's face, Milo whispered, "Peek-a-boo."

"He can see me?"

"I think he's impressed."

Rosy wings flared wide for balance as he leaned close. "I am here."

Stretching out one small hand, Zeke grabbed Ethan's nose. "'Onk."

ROUGH AND TUMBLE

STRANGERS IN THE KITCHEN

Ethan slipped into the kitchen earlier than usual, eager for a quiet chat with Lucan, but he drew up short just inside the door. Two strangers stood beside the table. They glanced up, and Ethan shuffled his feet, unsure how to proceed.

Bronze stitching marked them as Guardians. The one with black curls was impressively tall, even bigger than Othniel. With a series of shy glances, Ethan gained his first impressions—strong chin, crooked nose, heavy brows, and fine scars showing pale against olive skin.

Just then, Lucan entered the room, and a slow smile spread across his face. "Ah."

102
The Least of These

Ethan's eyes widened as the pieces fell into place. Two new Guardians had been Sent. Another baby would be born to the Pomeroy family. Zeke was going to be a big brother!

"You waited many years," Lucan was saying.

"Yes."

Since Ethan's appointment had come while he was still an adolescent, he'd remain the junior member of their Hedge, for the newcomer was full-grown—broad in the chest and battle-scarred. This warrior would add great strength and experience to their defenses.

With a wistful pang, Ethan realized that the new apprentice would be taking his former place at Lucan's side.

THE BIGGER THEY ARE

Unworthy feelings tumbled in Ethan's heart, but a still, small voice reminded, *'Your place is established. His place is assured. But he is in need of reassurance.'*

Suddenly able to see how ill-at-ease the newcomer was, he stepped forward. "I am Ethan, apprentice to Conrad."

"Alpheus, apprentice to Kin." Big fists clenched and unclenched, causing the dark blue bars of his furled wings to ripple with his muscles. When Alpheus offered his hand, Ethan's disappeared within its gentle grasp, which slowly shifted into a nervous cling.

Tightening his hold, Ethan turned to ask Lucan, "May I show him Zeke?"

104
AND THIS SHALL BE A SIGN

When Alpheus halted halfway up the stairs, Ethan turned to see what was wrong. Even standing two steps higher, he was still shorter than the newest member of the Hedge. "Yes?"

Alpheus quietly revealed, "I was told that the first one to reach out to me would need me."

"You were Sent to your charge … and to me?"

Alpheus nodded.

"Do you know why?"

He shook his head. "But you can count on my support."

Ethan sheepishly said, "Here I thought *you* might need *me*."

With a sudden smile, Alpheus asked, "How could I not rely upon my first friend?"

MATCH MADE IN HEAVEN

Alpheus stooped to enter the room where bunked beds and a crib shared space with a diaper changing table. Ethan automatically unfurled his wings and stretched them over his sleeping charge, their luminescence lending a rosy blush to his fair cheeks. "This is Zeke … short for Hezekiah."

"He's so *small*."

Ethan crossed his forearms on the crib rail, resting his chin on them as he looked down. "Yet he has grown so much."

"Is this what it's like?" Alpheus asked, his tone rich with wonder. "Do you love him?"

With a crooked smile, the younger Guardian repeated, "So much."

106
KEEN EDGE

Ethan nibbled slowly at his manna, extending his break for as long as possible. He and Raz had joined the long row of Messengers watching Alpheus's mentor train.

Liquid gold wings swirled around Kin's angular frame as he circled and spun, slinging knives with deadly accuracy. Swoop. *Cling.* Leap. *Clang.* Alpheus fended the barrage off with the flat of a broadsword that was taller than Ethan.

When they took a break for Kin to collect his weaponry, Ethan sidled up to Alpheus. "May I try your sword?"

He offered the hilt with a small smile. "Try."

Ethan couldn't budge it.

Ethan grunted with the effort of keeping Alpheus's ungainly weapon from dropping. The big warrior's laugh was a low-rolling, friendly sound that lifted Ethan's heart. Brightening, he glanced up and caught Kin's eye.

Alpheus's slim mentor didn't say anything, but his eyebrows waggled before settling in a lopsided quirk under black bangs.

Thinking back, Ethan realized that in all the days since this pair had joined the Hedge, he'd never heard Kin speak. "You are not very talkative."

"No?" Kin's tone was feather light. After some thought, he inclined his head and chin-length hair swept forward, brushing his jawline. "No."

108
Wake Up Call

The day Zeke staged an escape from his crib during naptime, Conrad and Ethan abandoned their training to rush to his side. As he drew breath to wail, four Guardians crammed into the bedroom and hovered around the frightened, fallen boy.

"I should have been here," Ethan mourned.

Alpheus guiltily murmured, "I *was* here."

"Don't fret. Zeke's fine," Conrad soothed as Naomi rushed in.

Lucan remarked, "She was sound asleep. Her strength has flagged."

"Heaven help me," the woman sighed. "How am I going to keep up with you *and* this one?"

"Ah," Lucan said with satisfaction. "She has realized."

Persistence, Pillows, and Plans

Zeke took a second tumble from his crib, and Naomi started stacking pillows beside his bed. When she applied to her mother-in-law for advice, Grandma Nell laughed. "The apple doesn't fall far from the tree. Jayce was the same."

"What did you do?"

"Me? Nothing that worked. It was Pete who put a stop to that youngster's shenanigans."

"How?"

The older woman frowned thoughtfully. "I wonder if he held onto it. He's one part sentimental and two parts pack rat."

As Naomi and Nell set out to find Grandpa Pete, Ethan trailed after … one part relieved and two parts mystified.

110
PUT A LID ON IT

Grandpa Pete's solution to the matter involved two-by-fours and chicken wire. Lowering the cover into place, he checked the fit, then nodded. "It's not pretty, but there's no sharp edges. And it's too heavy for the little rascal to budge."

Doubts creased Naomi's face. "It feels like we're putting him in a *cage*."

"All we're doing is keeping him safe," Jayce said, tickling the boy in his arms until he giggled. "Isn't this the third time he fell?"

"Fourth," she admitted with a wince.

"That settles it," decreed Jayce. "Zeke is now the main attraction in the Pomeroy family zoo!"

Temporary Measures

Ethan eased into the corner as the children crowded in.

"Zeke's in a zoo?" asked Neil. "Can I try?"

Tad clambered onto the top bunk. "You're too big for the crib."

"Then let Beau try it. He's still little."

"Am not," protested the six-year-old. But then he tugged at Jayce's pantleg. "Can I, Daddy?"

Soon, the brothers shared the makeshift cage. Naomi dissolved into smiles as Beau tried to teach Zeke how to roar. "It's not so bad. And it's only temporary."

Grandpa Pete chuckled. "He'll outgrow the crib and be into new kinds of trouble before you know it!"

112
WHISTLE IN THE WIND

Finding Alpheus wasn't too difficult. Ethan only needed to follow his ears. Trills and cascades, tremolos and warbles—the big warrior's whistling led Ethan unerringly to the old oak at the front of the property.

Leaves rattled in the icy wind, clinging stubbornly to spreading limbs despite the change in season. Sparrows and chickadees clustered in the nearest branches, as if listening.

Ethan waited for Alpheus to reach his tune's end before calling, "Naomi is bundling up Zeke for a trip into town. Ready to fly?"

Alpheus reached for the sword he'd propped in a forked branch above him. "Always."

113
BROKEN RECORD

Christmas was in the air—snow and spice, cedar and pine. Alpheus faced his first holiday with a steady sort of joy, but Ethan's days held no such peace.

"Momma! Have you seen Zeke?"

Naomi pulled gingerbread men out of the oven. "I thought you and Neil were playing with him."

Tad's shoulders hunched. "He got away from us."

"Zeke!" she called. "Where are you, little man?"

Ethan wished he could have warned her, but it was far too late.

Whoosh! Whump! Smash! Tinkle!

At the tender age of eighteen months, Zeke toppled the Christmas tree … and his father's record.

114
DOUBLING THE GUARD

Trumble approached Ethan late that night. "Lucan told me what happened today."

The young Guardian lowered his gaze.

"Alpheus offered to trade places with you in the rotation. So you can stay closer to Zeke."

Ethan's head snapped up.

Sighing softly, Trumble asked, "Do you envy his place?"

He slowly nodded.

"Are you aware how long Alpheus waited to be Sent?"

"Yes," Ethan whispered.

"I cannot ask him to give up his place."

"No," he agreed.

"But Lucan believes there is safety in numbers."

Ethan straightened, and Trumble chuckled. "Naomi needs all the help she can get. Go to Zeke."

The Brush of Angels' Wings

Ethan cringed inwardly as Zeke hip-hopped down the snowy porch steps, but they posed no real difficulty. However, the moment the toddler's boot hit the front sidewalk, shimmering wings knocked him onto his well-padded rump and sent him spinning. Ethan gawked at the culprits.

"No harm done," Lucan soothed.

"He's *fine*," promised Jomei.

Lucan nodded at the door. "More importantly, so is Naomi."

Ethan turned in time to see Jayce react to Zeke's spill. Slipping an arm protectively around his wife's waist and resting his other hand on the swell of her belly, he said, "Let's *not* follow Zeke's example."

116
Slippery When Wet

Spring arrived, and the great outdoors was once more a part of Zeke's days. Ethan leaned in the open doorway of the upstairs bathroom where his charge was enjoying a post-play bath under his mother's watchful eye.

"How can one boy accumulate so much dirt?" Ethan asked unheard.

The tub sported a dingy ring by the time Naomi wrapped her son in a towel. After some fluffing, Zeke's golden hair shone like a halo, but he was no angel. Giggling, the little boy slipped under his mother's arm and streaked down the hallway, naked as the day he was born.

Not So Alone

Ethan ranged into the depths of the orchard to practice. Yannis and Garrick had taken it into their heads to give him archery lessons, but he felt awkward handling the unfamiliar weapon. Nocking an arrow, he drew the borrowed bow, pulling at aches in muscles unused to such tension. "I do not think I was intended for this," he murmured.

"Intent. Contempt. Condemned."

A soft hiss of laughter clutched Ethan's heart. His arrow sheared off into the trees, and he bobbled the bow in his haste to draw his sword.

From another direction, the voice mocked, *"Fumble. Bumble. Stumble. Fall."*

118
Only a Voice

"*Namby pamby. Pampered poppet.*" The rasping chant was accompanied by an odd, creaking note.

Ethan whirled, trying to locate his attacker. Although it wasn't really an attack. Only a voice. "Where are you?"

"*Here.*"

"Show yourself!"

"*No, for I am ugly.*"

The young Guardian blinked. "Naturally."

"*Do you mock what I have become?*"

Ethan couldn't imagine doing so and shook his head. Warily adjusting his grip, he turned slowly. "Who are you?"

"*No one of consequence.*"

"Why are you hiding here?"

"*Why are you?*"

"I am not hiding. I am simply alone."

Laughter hissed anew. "*Yes, for I am nothing.*"

Unwelcome Parallels

"**F**ight me!"

"No, for I am harmless." After a considering pause, the Fallen added, *"Much like yourself."*

The remark stung more than it should have. Young. Small. Ethan often wondered why God had chosen one so new to guard a life as precious as Zeke's. "You do not belong here."

"Do you?"

"This is where I was Sent!"

"This is where I was Cast." The voice shifted, coming from behind him. *"So much alike. Wouldn't you agree?"*

Ethan pivoted, but saw no sign of his tormentor. "We have nothing in common."

"Wrong," he calmly countered. *"For we are both here."*

SLIPPING AWAY

"**Y**ou do not belong here!" Ethan repeated, sending Verrill a silent plea for help.

"You deny my place, yet I remain." The sing-song voice continued, *"You are the one out of place."*

"My place is assured."

"Once again, we are the same." Ethan spun as the Fallen's call came more softly. *"Will you chase me? Let me lead you."*

Ethan caught sight of members from his Flight circling. "Wait!"

"Why?"

"Your name," Ethan blurted, wanting to hold him back. "Do you have one?"

With rough-edged sweetness, he replied, *"No, for it was blotted out. But you may call me Blight."*

VERIFYING THE MESSAGE

Ethan slumped on the floor in the kitchen next to Zeke's play pen, Verrill sitting quietly at his side. The Messenger soothed, "Peace, friend. You found him. To think, the Fallen actually took such a name."

"To be honest, he found me." With a sidelong glance at his teammate, he asked, "What do I do?"

"Cut him out," Verrill reminded. "Before he bears the fruit of destruction."

"But how?" Ethan asked in a low voice. "How can I catch what I cannot see?"

The Messenger's brown hands fluttered. "Sounds like the riddle of faith. Perhaps faith will give you sight."

122
HERE, KITTY, KITTY

The Pomeroy children had been coming and going all morning, but Zeke hardly noticed the slap of the screen door. His mother had given him an assortment of pots, lids, and spoons to play with, and the boy was completely absorbed.

Until a curious kitten slipped inside.

Ethan saw a spark kindle in Zeke's blue eyes when he spotted the barncat. One pudgy hand thrust out between the rails of his playpen as he called, "Kiddy, kiddy, kiddy …?"

A pulled tail. A cat's yowl. A scratched hand. A baby's wail. Both youngsters were a little wiser for their encounter.

HEAD FOR THE HALLS

On Sunday morning, Zeke escaped the church nursery, making a beeline for the back stairs. Ethan gave chase, but thankfully, his charge didn't make it far.

"Well, well!" Milo sat on the top step, hands open. "Can you climb?"

Zeke thumped his way up to the mailman.

"Remember me?"

Stretching high, Zeke grabbed Milo's nose.

He obliged with a cheerful, "Honk!"

The boy was all smiles when Milo scooped him up, saying, "Let's go find your daddy before Ethan flutters to bits."

Ethan trailed after them. "Thank you, Milo."

The Messenger's voice reached gently into his mind. *"Any time, friend."*

124
Learning the Hard Way

Ethan often intervened in Zeke's life, preventing tiny tragedies from playing out. But one day, while skidding across the floor, arm outstretched to cushion a fall, a voice urged, *'Let him fall, my tenderhearted one.'*

He quickly snatched back his hand, and Zeke hit the ground. Hard.

After a stunned silence, the little guy's face crumpled, and Ethan's heart clenched painfully.

Later, Conrad nodded sympathetically, but said, "God is wise. Let the boy taste the consequences of his actions so he can learn from them. It's part of growing up."

"For him or for me."

Conrad replied, "You're growing together."

In the Fullness of Time

Alpheus stretched out on the boys' bedroom floor, adding bass notes to Trumble's and Ethan's bright harmony. A second bunk bed now stood against the far wall, in readiness for the Pomeroys' expanding family. Naomi's due date had come and gone, and tensions were running high.

A sudden *thud* from the next room silenced the trio, and a moment later, Jomei slipped into the room. "It's time. Alpheus …? Did he *faint*?"

Ethan patted the big warrior's cheek. "I believe so!"

Trumble chuckled. "Good thing he was already on the floor. I would sooner try to catch a toppling tower."

126
CARRIED AWAY

Alpheus blinked back to consciousness, and Ethan smiled down at him. "On your feet, Guardian. Your time has come."

Kin joined them, crouching beside his apprentice. Eyebrows quirking, he asked, "Ready?"

"I thought so, but I'm no longer sure," Alpheus confessed.

In the end, Othniel and Taweel had to carry their teammate as they chased Jayce's minivan toward the highway and the hospital.

Ethan nudged Conrad. "Was I *that* nervous?"

"Knock-kneed and crumple-winged," his mentor assured. "No Guardian can keep his composure when meeting the one he was created to love."

"Then this is as it should be?"

"Every time."

Welcome to the Family

Ethan slipped into the hospital room where Jayce shepherded his children. "Come meet your new brother!"

"Can I hold him?" Prissie asked.

"Sure, sure. Everyone gets a turn!"

"Momma," Tad greeted, propping his elbows on the mattress at the foot of the bed.

Neil pushed closer, trying to see inside the blue blanket. "Does he look like me?"

"Or me?" asked Beau.

While the Pomeroys talked, Ethan marveled at Alpheus's wingspan. Deep blue folds extended far enough to encompass the entire family. The Guardian's qualms had vanished, leaving joy and peace … and an unwavering gaze for his newborn charge.

128
Baby Mine

Jayce boosted Zeke onto the bed, and he stared in amazement at the baby, as if it had never occurred to his young mind that the baby everyone had talked about was actually going to come.

"Mine?"

"Yes, Zeke," his father replied. "This is your new brother."

"Baby?"

Jayce patiently answered, "Yes, Zeke. He's your baby brother."

The boy crawled to his mother's side and carefully patted the newborn's fuzz of dark hair. Looking up into his mother's face, he whispered, "Baby."

"Yes, Zeke. He's our baby." Trading a long look with her husband, Naomi revealed, "His name is Jude."

TERRIBLY TWO

Just two weeks later, Zeke celebrated his second birthday. For his son's milestone, Jayce created a tower of cupcakes on tiered cake plates. They made a festive display, and Ethan could tell that this time around, his charge understood that something special was happening. The small pile of brightly-wrapped presents. The boisterous birthday song. Tad's patient coaching for the candle-blowing. When Zeke was granted two cupcakes, one from each parent, he did the only sensible thing.

He smashed them together.

Amidst all the laughter, Jayce said, "And so it begins. Something tells me Zeke is going to be terribly two!"

130
NEED FOR SPEED

Ethan decided that Jayce and Naomi were far braver than he. Instead of trying to prevent their young son from feats of derring-do, they equipped him for more.

The young guardian watched with considerable trepidation as Grandpa Pete wheeled Zeke's final birthday present out from behind a stack of crates in the apple barn. Amidst cheers and encouragement, the two-year-old clambered aboard. Tad and Neil each grabbed the red trike's handles and raced him across the cement floor.

Grandpa Pete beamed. "Keep him busy. That's the trick."

Naomi cuddled Jude close, smiling. "He's so happy!"

Zeke chortled. "Faster! More faster!"

LINES ON THE WALL

Before bedtime, Jayce recorded Zeke's height with an orange marker on the laundry room wall.

Later, Ethan knelt in the narrow space to study the inscriptions. Conrad asked, "Well?"

"Tad will always be taller than Neil."

"Where does Zeke fall?"

Ethan replied, "He nearly makes Tad's mark, but I think he was up on his toes."

"And you?"

Standing, he touched the highest line on the wall. Although small by Guardian standards, Ethan was still taller than Jayce.

"Thought so," Conrad pointedly looked *up* into his apprentice's widening eyes. "You're so often with Alpheus, it's no wonder we didn't notice."

132
QUACK, QUACK

Ethan was taking his refreshment when duty called.

"Quack! Quack! Quack!"

Raz laughed as he bundled away their manna boxes. "Isn't Zeke supposed to be napping in his cage?"

"Naomi moved him into the bottom bunk," Ethan explained. "He does not always stay."

"Quack!" Zeke trotted along after his grandfather's ducks. "Wabble, wabble wabble!"

Under the fence. Down the path. The boy was up to his knees in the duck pond before Ethan could hook his finger through a belt loop.

"Help is on the way," Raz promised.

Tad jogged over and groaned, "Oh, *Zeke*."

Ethan couldn't have agreed more.

Up, Down, In, Around

Seven-year-old Beau kept track of Tuesdays because storytime at their local library was the highlight of his week.

Zeke enjoyed these outings just as much as his brother, but not for books' sake. *His* fascination lay in the gazebo where storytime was held. Stairs, benches, lattice, rails—they were better than any jungle gym.

Lucan asked, "Inside or the outside?"

With a rueful smile, Ethan replied, "I will leave the perimeter to you."

Naomi's Guardian scanned the vicinity. "Ah."

"What?"

"He is gone."

Several other children's guardians helpfully pointed the way. Somehow, Zeke had found his way *under* the gazebo.

Me, Mysewf, and Mine

By summer's end, Zeke had mastered pedaling his trike and was ready to test his limits. Ethan paced after the boy as he struggled determinedly along the gravel road.

Thankfully, eight-year-old Prissie hurried over. "No-no, Zeke! Not in the road!"

He pouted. "Daddy."

"The bakery's too far," his sister insisted. "Do you need help back to the driveway?"

"Mysewf."

"Are you sure?"

"Mysewf."

While Prissie watched her brother grind his way back onto the driveway, Milo arrived with the mail, and Zeke tumbled off his trike in a rush. "My 'Lo!"

Ethan grinned when the Messenger cheerfully replied, "My 'Eke!"

  ROUGH AND TUMBLE

PARODY OF SONGS

Ethan enjoyed the busyness of harvest, when so many Flights converged on the Pomeroys' farm. With so many Guardians on hand, you'd think there was no safer place. But Ethan couldn't lapse into a false sense of security. One enemy was too close for any comfort.

He couldn't fathom why the rest were deaf to Blight's hissing whispers. They came at all hours, drifting from odd corners, slinking from the shadows. Stray comments. Little jokes. Random asides. Litanies of grievances that reminded Ethan uncomfortably of evensong.

If such a thing was possible, Ethan would have guessed that Blight was lonely.

136
DAY OF REST

On an autumn Sunday that was summer-warm, Jayce packed a lunch and led his lot into the orchard. The children ran ahead, shouting suggestions for picnic spots, and their Guardians followed, sketching lazy circles over the treetops.

Climbing trees. Running races. Playing catch. Telling stories.

Later, Ethan knelt beside Alpheus, who watched over naptime. Naomi snoozed on a soft, plaid blanket, Zeke tucked against one side, Jude on the other. Alpheus's expression was peaceful, and he kept his voice low. "I like this kind of lull."

"So do they," Ethan replied, gazing fondly at Zeke's rumpled repose. "We all do."

Alpheus's hands tightened into fists as he hovered next to the table, wings aflutter. "What should we do?"

Ethan admitted, "I am uncertain. Lucan, will this harm him?"

"He seems to be enjoying the attention," the silver-eyed Guardian remarked.

"B-but …!" Alpheus stammered.

Applesauce had been a staple of Zeke's diet for quite some time. But it was a little early for it to be part of Jude's. Short of direct intervention, Ethan had no idea how to stop Zeke from spooning more into his baby brother's mouth.

Lucan chuckled. "Jude is content. Zeke is entertained. Let them … bond."

138
Parental Stake Out

Someone had been snitching from the old-fashioned pie safe where Naomi kept Christmas goodies. The older kids protested their innocence, leaving one impossibility.

"He's *two*." Jayce whispered. "There's no way!"

Naomi shushed him as Zeke showed up in footie pajamas. A stockpot for a step stool. A rat tail comb for a lock-pick. When the boy trotted from the room munching a gingerbread man, Ethan was startled by a low chuckle.

Jayce exclaimed, "My son's an evil genius!"

Naomi thumped his arm. "Don't sound so proud!"

Still grinning, Jayce helped his wife up. "Let's go end Zeke's life of crime."

139
Cuddle Buddy

Jude was a born cuddler. He couldn't be happier than when he was nestled in the crook of someone's arm, and he was happiest if they were smiling back at him. This kept Naomi's hands full in a new way, making Jayce chief Zeke-wrangler.

Zeke was a born climber. The moment his father came into view, he was running, reaching, and clambering his way onto the man's shoulders.

Jomei remarked, "That boy wants nothing more or less than to be smack dab in the middle of Jayce's life."

Ethan looked on approvingly. "Giving full attention, and demanding it in return."

"There are times when I think he's still a child," Jomei said. "At least at heart."

"Is that not good?" Ethan checked. "God cherishes a child-like faith."

"There's faith," conceded Jayce's Guardian. "And then, there's play."

The man had brought his two-and-a-half-year-old son into work with him, and Zeke had spotted the gingerbread house in the bakery window. His fascination was immediate. Rather than risk its destruction, Jayce was helping his son build a smaller version. Icing, crumbs, candy, and patience dribbled everywhere.

"A solid tactic," said Ethan.

Jomei's gaze was on his charge's face. "A masterpiece in the making."

FEVERED DREAMS

"**H**ow is he?"

Ethan met Raz's question with a soulful gaze and sad headshake.

"Poor tyker. But I got the go-ahead for something that'll make you *both* feel better." The Messenger's green eyes sparkled. "Meetcha in dreams!"

Moments later, Ethan stepped onto an endless lawn where Zeke chased colored balls of varying sizes. The little boy noticed him and trotted over.

Ethan knelt to ask, "Can I play, too?"

"Up!" Zeke demanded, hands lifted.

Ethan suspected Zeke was after his sword. He unfurled his wings, eager to show the boy just how high *up* could go.

Joy soared 'til morning.

142
ALPHEUS AND THE KITTENS

irds often flocked to Alpheus, who whistled melodies around their twittering. But Ethan hadn't realized he was equally fond of small animals … until the day he found Alpheus in the hayloft with a lapful of kittens.

Smiling at his friend's embarrassment, Ethan asked, "What happened?"

After a lengthy pause, Alpheus admitted, "Nothing."

Ethan plopped down and tickled one of the babies under its chin. Wide blue eyes. Pink pads on tiny paws. The littlest one squeaked, then a rumble started, like the sputter of a tiny engine.

Ethan wryly murmured, "Heaven's mighty warriors …"

Alpheus concluded, "… teaching kittens to purr."

SERIOUSLY FUN

Early summer thundershowers found the Pomeroy children riding bikes—and trike—in the apple barn while cherubim cavorted in the rafters.

"Over, then under?" suggested Yannis.

Garrick countered, "Or under, then over?"

"Both could be tricky."

"But near misses make things more exciting!"

Ethan contemplated the obstacle course Neil was setting up on the floor below. Visible and invisible were in sync. He glanced at his teammates. "May I play?"

Yannis gasped in affront. "This is no *game*!"

"We take our training *very* seriously," Garrick agreed.

Ethan smiled softly.

The archers traded a look, then laughed. "Over, under, *and through*!"

144
GUARD AND PROTECT

After evensong, Conrad approached Tycho. "There's an informal tradition among Guardians …?"

"Go on," invited the lean archer.

"When a child marks three years, three voices rise in song—Guardian, mentor, and captain."

"When?"

Ethan stepped forward. "Zeke's birthday is tomorrow, so … tonight?"

Within the hour, they gathered inside the farmhouse, and Tycho considered the youngster in the bottom bunk. "I protect people in a general sense. Your task is more personal."

Fingertips brushing Zeke's mop, Ethan looked to his captain. "Tonight, we will share."

Conrad smirked. "Stand guard with us, Protector. Sing for joy over one small boy."

That summer, First Baptist Church's congregation invited Milo Leggett to teach Sunday school. Beau Pomeroy was excited to be part of his class, but Prissie was vocal in her disappointment. "I'm the right age!"

"You're a girl, Priss," Neil drawled. "Milo teaches the boys' class."

"No fair!"

Zeke sidled up and suggested, "Change."

"They won't let me change classes."

Ethan could see what Zeke had behind his back, and it worried him.

"Nope," Zeke countered. "Change to a boy! I'll help!"

Scissors snipped thin air as Prissie shrieked and ran.

Beau disarmed the would-be barber; Neil was too busy laughing.

146
MASON JARS

The children were chasing fireflies on the front lawn. Prissie lectured. Beau pounced. Zeke ran in circles, hands in the air. And on the porch, three mason jars became lanterns. Prissie's had four fireflies; Beau's held five. Only Zeke's remained unlit.

Until a curious yahavim tiptoed over for a closer look. With a flick of translucent wings, Omri investigated Zeke's jar from the inside.

"Should we call him back?" Ethan asked.

Taweel grunted. "There is no danger."

Given Zeke's prowess, he was probably right. Yet the little boy's jar glowed more brightly than its neighbors. Luminous with Omri's innocent delight.

SODA MACHINE

"This way. This way." Zeke led his baby brother by the hand, right into the corner store.

Leaning over the counter, the owner remarked, "Jude can walk now."

Zeke grinned. "Real good. So we're shopping."

The man stroked his moustache, eyes on the door. "That so?"

Showing off two quarters, the boy pointed to the soda machine humming in the corner. "We're gonna share."

"Be our guest." The owner watched like a hawk as the brothers completed their mission. Then he beckoned his wife over. "Got us some runaways."

"I'll be!" With an indulgent smile, she murmured, "Best call Jayce."

148

LITTLE BOY BLUE

Zeke failed to show up at dinnertime, so his family searched the farm from barns to back forty. The whole while, Conrad and Ethan stood guard over the boy's hiding place. "Can we do *anything*?" Ethan asked. "They are afraid."

"Perhaps we can … *hint*." Pointing to Prissie, Conrad suggested, "Catch her eye."

"How?"

Conrad smirked. "She likes pink."

With an earnest hope that God would allow Prissie a glimpse of invisible things, Ethan unfurled his wings, scattering fallen leaves across the lawn. She turned, her gaze fixing on the leaf pile Zeke had worn himself out making.

"Found him!"

The orchard whirled with activity. Ethan was intrigued that the Pomeroys resorted to an almost angelic system to keep track of everyone. Two-by-two.

Zeke's mentor was thirteen-year-old Tad. Slow-and-steady met rough-and-tumble … and struck a balance. There was no use trying to keep Zeke out of the trees, so Tad showed his little brother where to put his feet so he wouldn't damage the leaflets that would produce next year's crop. By day's end, Zeke scampered through swaying treetops, and his partner casually caught the apples he dropped.

Big brothers made decent Guardians. Someday, Ethan intended to tell Tad so.

150
CHEERING SECTION

That year, Neil was fitted for pads and cleats, and the Hedge members took to calling him their little warrior. The Pomeroys flocked to the boy's support. Playing catch. Team colors. Pep talks. Tickets to the high school home games.

Football introduced Zeke to marching bands, concession stands, and *big* bleachers. Ethan assumed this would lead to new levels of mischief, but the upshot startled him. While Jayce cheered on Neil, Zeke stuck close … and watched closer.

Ethan was stumped. "What *is* he planning?"

"Zeke wants his father's admiration," Jomei replied wisely. "He's probably planning to distinguish himself. Somehow."

Grandma Nell didn't notice the time as she and Naomi worked through the pre-Thanksgiving baking.

Ethan sympathized with Zeke. Lunch was late.

Bringing footstools to the coffee table, Zeke sat Jude down before bringing two purple plastic spoons from Prissie's tea set. Next … an entire pumpkin pie. The brothers started in the middle.

Alpheus chuckled when Jude dropped his spoon and resorted to feeding himself by the handful.

Shortly thereafter, Naomi ran for her camera, and Grandma Nell laughed through an apology. "I'll make you a good, big dinner tonight, sweetie."

Zeke patted his stomach, smiling. "Nope! All full!"

When the Good News is shared, angels gather. The family room slowly filled as Zeke shared part of the Story with his baby brother.

Naomi had a battered nativity set, perfect for little hands, one the kids could play with. Jude calmly chewed on a camel's ear while Zeke narrated the events of the first Christmas, moving the figurines as he talked. His enthusiasm brought a smile to Ethan's face.

"Zeke expresses himself well," Lucan decreed.

Jomei nodded. "The embellishments are … interesting."

"Gold Edition Wise Men?" Othniel scoffed.

"Named Frank, Cents, and Murray," Jomei blandly added.

Ethan laughed sheepishly.

 ROUGH AND TUMBLE

153
FOURTHBORN SON

Ethan wasn't sure if Zeke loved the bakery because his father was there … or because Jayce let him experiment in the kitchen. The young Guardian leaned on the table, chin on his fist as he watched the little boy. In an apron several sizes too big, Zeke tried to emulate his father's kneading technique.

"Zeke learns by doing."

"Jayce has noticed. Perhaps *this* boy will follow in his footsteps." Jomei leaned against the far wall, arms folded over his chest, looking on with an equally contented smile as his charge passed on a love for baking to his son.

154
Too Quiet

"He is being very careful," Ethan whispered, wondering if he could safely intervene.

Alpheus snorted. "He's always quiet when he gets into mischief."

"Jude is very brave."

"Too young. Too trusting," grumbled the big Guardian as he flexed his hands.

Ethan bit his lip. "He is in *so* much trouble."

"Undoubtedly." Tipping his head to one side, Alpheus said, "It's an interesting look. You should try it."

"Me?" The younger warrior ruffled up short bristles. "I would rather not let Zeke near my hair."

As more crinkle-edged tufts of brown hair hit the floor, Alpheus added, "Especially with pinking shears."

"So much for childproofing," Naomi sighed, poking at the plastic latch that had been no match for her young son.

Zeke beamed. "I helped!"

Ethan looked on curiously as Naomi quietly collected bottles—bubble bath, body wash, shampoo, conditioner, lotion, bath oil beads, and a sprinkling of salts. While she tidied up, she made her expectations clear. "No more mixing without Momma."

"'Kay!"

Starting the water, she helped him swish the goop into a towering, fragrant foam. "Just wait until your father gets a whiff of you, little man!"

"Pretty!" Zeke boasted.

She wrinkled her nose. "Like a perfume factory."

156
TAMPERING

"*Simple ploys. Careless boys.*"

Blight's sing-song chant drifted like a fitful breeze. A puff here, a gust there. Impossible to pin down. But Ethan gave chase, jaw clenched, sword ready.

"*Broken toys. Funny noise.*"

Even from here, on the fringes of the orchard behind the machine shed, the Guardian could hear his charge's sobs. Zeke was suffering. Lucan feared a break. Conrad warned of stitches.

"You!" Ethan shouted, tumultuous emotions causing his voice to crack. "You are responsible! I know it was you!"

A hiss of laughter trickled down the young warrior's spine. "*What the Faithful enjoys, the Fallen destroys!*"

HARSH TRUTHS

"*Y*ou shake. You quake.*" Blight's gentle mockery shifted, seeming to come from above, below, behind. Pigeons scattered, and a rabbit leapt from its burrow, streaking away. *"Are you angry with me ... or yourself?"*

Ethan winced. Was Zeke hurting because he'd failed to get rid of this threat?

"He breaks. He bleeds," crooned the demon. *"But <u>we</u> are not to blame."*

"You *knew* he would not be able to resist!"

"He chose; he fell." His tone turned flinty. "These are just consequences."

Choked by anger, rattled by regrets, Ethan was unprepared for what happened next.

Blight stepped into the open.

158
ℓULLED

Ethan had formed numerous impressions of the person standing before him. Clever. Cautious. Blight was given to acerbic remarks. Bitter. Ironic. Had Ethan grown too accustomed to his quarry's voice? Passive. Patient. He stared guardedly at one whose light had gone dim. Slender. Smiling. Any sense of security had clearly been false. "You are my enemy."

Lusterless black hair hung around bony shoulders. Pointed ears and frayed stitching marked him as a former Observer. Blight stared back with eyes in a shade of blue that hinted at former glories. Lively. Lovely.

Shaking his head, Blight replied, "I am your secret."

I AND THEE

No one else in the Hedge knew a demon dwelt in the orchard, but Blight made it sound as if Ethan was harboring an enemy. "You misunderstand."

"You listen. You linger." Blight glided closer. "You *like* me."

Ethan blanched. "You are Fallen. I am Faithful."

"An interesting contrast. An insider and an outcast." His eyes glittered. "We should explore our differences."

The invitation was unthinkable. Shaking his head, the young Guardian retreated. "There is no *we*."

"No?" Blight laughed. "I and thee have been a *we* since you were Sent to me."

Conrad was calling. Zeke was leaving. Ethan fled.

160
GET WELL SOON

During his fourth birthday festivities, Zeke sported a florescent green cast plastered with stickers and scrawled wishes for a quick recovery. Late that night, Ethan waited beside the boy's bed for Raz. "All set!" the Messenger exclaimed, presenting him with a pilfered permanent marker.

They chose the best spot, right under the boy's elbow. Zeke would never see, let alone interpret heaven's language, but Ethan felt better adding his own note. Raz crowded close. Ethan bit his lip and, with excruciating care, formed three words—*I am here.*

Finding the sentiment lacking, he added a lopsided heart … and smiled.

Once Upon a Bedtime

*T*hump. *Whump.*

Ethan's eyes widened, and he raised one wing to deflect a pillow.

Patter. Clatter. Thud.

Alpheus's low chuckle deepened into a rolling laugh.

Kerfuffle. Kerflop.

Jayce's growl cut off at the sound of feet on the stairs.

Shush. Hush. Hurry.

By the time Naomi arrived, father and sons were crowded together on the bed. Blankets askew. Lampshade tilted. Expressions angelic.

"What are you three doing?" she asked suspiciously.

Jayce cheerfully replied, "Bedtime stories."

Jude giggled.

When Zeke helpfully took the book out of his father's hands and turned it right-side up, Ethan covered his eyes, and Alpheus guffawed.

162
WILD BLACKBERRIES

Purple juices stained Zeke's fingers and dribbled down his chin.

Prissie wailed, "No fair! Now there's not enough for a pie!"

Tad took his little brother's hand. "I'll bring Zeke home. You start filling the pail again."

Neil pouted. "How come you're skipping out?"

"Don't worry. I'll do my part." Tad started walking.

"M'sorry," Zeke mumbled, shuffling along.

"I bet," his oldest brother said. "Can you make it?"

"Nuh-uh."

Tad steered toward a stump. "Stick to eating what you pick yourself. That's fair. And stop eating *before* the good goes bad. Like now."

Zeke nodded, groaned, and emptied his stomach.

163
SLOPPING THE PIGS

The day Zeke's cast was removed, Grandpa Pete gruffly announced that a boy who'd turned four was man enough to help out around the farm.

To Ethan's chagrin, Zeke immediately begged, "Can I drive the tractor?"

"Not just yet," the old man replied.

"Rototiller? Mower?"

"*No!*" his grandfather exclaimed before gentling his tones. "Let's start with slop pails and nest boxes."

A few minutes later, Ethan flew in lazy circles above the lane to the back forty. Partnered with Tad, Zeke was giggling happily … sitting on his big brother's lap … steering the quad while Tad managed the accelerator.

164
ŁITTLE RED HEN

"**Z**eke has far more courage than I," Ethan said with a sigh. "I fled from Blight; he faces Bertha."

Raz leaned through the chicken coop door, then whistled. "Fourth showdown!"

Bertha was a mean old biddie with a comb that flopped to one side. Fluffing up her feathers, she glared at the newly-appointed egg thief.

"I'm bigger'n you," Zeke declared. "And your peck ain't so bad." Pulling on one of his grandpa's work gloves, he shielded the bare hand he slipped under the broody hen.

Raz offered a smattering of applause for Zeke, whose ingenuity left him four eggs richer.

Guilty Conscience

Ethan stood by with a pained expression as Zeke conducted an experiment. He dropped eggs one after another onto the barn's cement floor, where they landed with a satisfying *splat*.

"Not good," his Guardian sighed.

It wasn't something the boy had been specifically told not to do, but Zeke checked the barn door at intervals. His conscience was pricking. But not hard enough to keep him from climbing into the loft for some *extreme* egg-dropping.

Everything came to a screeching halt when Prissie arrived.

While she ran to tattle, Zeke considered the works of his hands and sighed, "*Not* good."

166
ZEKE AND JASPER

During the usual hubbub of a potluck Sunday, Ethan trailed after Zeke and fellow four-year-old, Jasper Reece, a sturdy boy with dark skin and big, brown eyes. They snuck into the hushed sanctuary; muffled giggles soon accompanied a convoluted—and rule-bending—game of chase.

When Jayce found them, they were a mess. Shirts untucked. Shoes missing. But Jayce didn't scold.

"I'm not in trouble?" Zeke asked bluntly.

"Church isn't just for sermons and songs. It's fellowship, and that means having fun with friends." Grinning boyishly, he invited, "How about second desserts?"

On their way out, Jasper whispered, "Your dad's cool."

ROUGH AND TUMBLE

RITE OF PASSAGE

Ethan remembered the Forgers presenting him with his first boots. Conrad nudged him, remarking, "Zeke's as bad as you were with lacing."

"He *will* master the task."

Jayce patiently demonstrated the crossing of loops. Neil followed suit too quickly to follow, but Tad and Beau slowly formed respectable double-knots.

With scrunchy-faced concentration, Zeke did his best. "Like this?"

"Sure, sure," his father agreed. "Don't the rest of you agree?"

"Fair's fair," Neil said. "He can come along."

Ethan blinked. "Where are they going?"

Conrad smirked as Zeke tromped inside, showing off his hand-me-down hiking boots. "Look, Momma! I'm goin' *camping*!"

168
Keepers of the Peace

Ethan sat with Trumble in the branches overshadowing the Pomeroys' campsite. The young warrior remarked, "We are perilously close to the battlelines, yet all is peaceful. Have the Fallen withdrawn from these woods because the Encampment is near?"

"Even with two legions of the heavenly host to oppose them, the enemy attacks whenever the impulse takes them." Trumble gestured to the campfire Jayce was building. "But for the sake of two park rangers, the Fallen scatter like sparks and vanish like smoke."

"Are these rangers men of prayer?"

"Makers of mountains, shepherds of stars," Trumble hinted.

Ethan's eyes widened. "Caretakers!"

Full Day

After one full day, Ethan's charge was mud-spattered, mosquito-bitten, and blissfully happy. Zeke had pine needles in his hair, burrs on his socks, and smoke in his eyes as he crowded close to the fire, watching blisters form on the skin of the hotdog skewered on his forked stick.

There were many things Ethan wished he could do—swat bugs, strengthen seams, and scoot the boy back about a foot from the flames. But he settled for stretching his wings forward until their pink folds swirled around Zeke's shoulders like a mantle. Which left Ethan bright-eyed, light-hearted, and blissfully happy.

170
Safe from Bears

Long before dawn, a tent unzipped, and Zeke crawled out. Ethan sighed and said, "You should go back to bed."

"How come?" Zeke rubbed his eyes. "Is there bears?"

The young Guardian hesitated. "Zeke?"

"Uh-huh?"

Ethan's heart thudded, but he managed a steady voice. "It is very late."

"Uh-huh." Reaching one hand toward the starry sky, he mumbled, "Moon's little."

"It seems so."

"Is there bears?" Zeke pressed.

"No."

"'Kay. 'Cause I gotta go."

After the boy relieved himself, Ethan coaxed, "Please, return to your father's side."

"Uh-huh."

"… I love you, Zeke."

Before the zipper fully closed, he whispered, "'Kay."

171
HOOK, LINE, AND SINKER

"Keep your eyes on that bobber," Jayce said, dropping his line into the river next to Zeke's. "If it gives a wiggle, you'll know you have a nibble."

The little boy lifted his bamboo pole to check on his worm. "When I catch a fish, will you eat it?"

"Sure, sure," Jayce agreed. "I'm famished!"

Minutes ticked by, and the young fisherman was losing interest. Until the bobber dipped.

Zeke yelped and yanked. His catch flipped and flashed. Before Jayce could grab the line, his lunch slapped him upside the head … and an exuberant Zeke was hooked on fishing.

172
Leaves of Three, Let them Be

Ethan was trying to think of a way to avert disaster when someone said, "Excuse me, young camper."

Both Zeke and his Guardian turned to see a balding park ranger with wire-rimmed glasses. "We should talk," the man said, clasping his hands behind his back.

"About what?" Zeke shuffled his feet. "Am I in trouble?"

"No, but I think it's time for a short lesson on the perils of poison ivy."

Several yahavim flitted around Ethan's head. With a gasp, he realized what their presence meant. "You are a Caretaker!"

Ranger Ochs spared him a glance. And a solemn wink.

"You can stand guard out here," Jomei offered kindly. "Jayce won't let anything happen to the boy."

Gazing steadily through the tunnel's entrance, Ethan said, "I belong with Zeke."

In the cave's depths, the guide invited everyone to experience complete darkness. Flashlights clicked off. Ethan bit his lip. This was no place for a child of light.

Suddenly, fingers brushed Ethan's knuckles, and he started. Zeke must have been reaching for his father, but the boy's small hand was soon nestled in his guardian angel's grasp.

It was hard to say which of them took more courage from the connection.

174
SOME MORE

Fine fish scales still stuck to Zeke's upper arms under a sheen of bug spray. Dirt from the caves, scum from the pond, ash from the campfire—Ethan doubted Zeke could get any grimier. Until Jayce produced two bags of marshmallows.

Tad was a roaster, patiently turning his stick above glowing embers until they were golden brown and gooey.

Zeke mimicked the technique long enough to get pearly strings of marshmallow stuck to everything, then switched to the torch method. Sooty flakes of blackened sugar. Dribbles of melting chocolate. Cracker crumbs galore. Two bags were barely enough. Everyone wanted s'more.

MISSED AND MISSING OUT

When the campers returned home and dragged themselves up the sidewalk, Naomi kissed each grubby boy, then her husband. "It's been too quiet without you."

Grandma Nell upheld a longstanding family tradition. Handing them each a fresh bar of soap, she promised, "I *will* be checking behind your ears."

Zeke surprised them all—Ethan included—when he bolted past everyone, practically tackling Jude. The two-year-old grabbed hold and giggled as Zeke gushed, "Tadpoles! Worms! Fish! Fire! Marshmallows! Only no bears, but that's okay." Zeke's sunburned, freckled nose bumped his younger brother's. "Hurry up and grow, Jude! You *gotta* see camping!"

FRATERNITY

That evening, two little boys crowded together in the sofa's corner. Jude hugged a stuffed lion, and Zeke turned the pages of a picture book, making up his own story to go with the illustrations. By and by, they nodded, yawned, and sagged together in sleep.

Naomi smiled and murmured, "Isn't that the sweetest thing? They missed each other."

A slow smile spread across Lucan's face. "Ah," he agreed, but his gaze was fixed on the two Guardians crowded together behind the sofa.

Ethan and Alpheus were a picture of contentment as they harmonized their way through a lilting lullaby.

Ethan wasn't the only one who noticed Zeke's hovering. Naomi tousled the boy's hair and asked, "After I put Jude down for his nap, would you help me in the garden?"

Zeke blinked. "No nap?"

"I'll postpone it if you'll help me pick beans."

"Sure!"

As they worked their way around trellises, Naomi asked, "What's on your mind, little mister?"

"Daddy."

"Oh?"

"He *needs* me."

"When did you notice this?"

"At camping," Zeke confided.

His mother asked, "Does this change things for you?"

"Yep. Gonna bake."

"Instead of …?"

Zeke bravely sacrificed his dream. "I was gonna have a circus."

178
PUTTING DOWN ROOTS

Naomi accepted a boy's need to break loose, shout, climb, and conquer, but these things were best done *outside*. And Zeke was ready. Ethan paid close attention while both parents laid out boundaries—literal and figurative. So long as Zeke stayed within those, he had the run of the place.

"Sound good?" asked Jayce.

"Yep!" Zeke replied, rushing out the door.

Dirt could wash out, but memories needed to work their way in. Jayce understood, just like his father before him. When you knew every inch of a place because you'd spent your childhood tromping through it, you loved it.

Ethan stayed close to Zeke during his first solo foray into the orchard, especially since Blight's light and laughing voice followed them through the trees. *"Dogging his steps. Darkening his door."*

Zeke scanned the trees, pausing from time to time to inspect one more closely. Finally, the boy clambered into one that suited his needs. A fork formed the perfect niche, and Zeke settled down, arms behind his head, gazing through the leaves toward the clear blue sky.

"This is good," he announced. "My own spot."

"Come out. Come back. Come here." With a dark chuckle, Blight added, *"Come alone."*

180
POLISHING APPLES

In preparation for the Milton County Fair, Jayce Pomeroy was making caramel apples. Zeke was his apple-washer, but the four-year-old wasn't satisfied. "Can I dip?"

"No." His father lifted a skewered apple from the double boiler of melted caramel, giving it an expert twirl before adding it to the long rows on the counters. The bell over the bakery's front door jangled, and Jayce hurried through the swinging door, saying, "Keep washing. We need that whole bushel."

Zeke hopped off his stool and pulled it over to the stove. Ethan groaned. "Do not disobey."

A stretch. A bump. Another catastrophe.

Red Handed

Ethan unfurled his wings quickly enough to keep the tumbling bowl of hot caramel from splattering Zeke, but the pan of boiling water under it was another matter.

Jayce tended his son's burned hand in silence, exuding more calm than Ethan could manage. Pink wings shuddered with every falling tear and hiccupping sob. Then the baker turned to the floor—scooping, scraping, and scrubbing.

Finally, Jayce straightened, hooking his thumbs into his apron. "Does it still hurt?"

The boy hugged his injured hand to his heart. "Very bad."

Ethan's breath caught when he realized Zeke wasn't replying. He was confessing.

182
CLEAR

"Show me where it hurts."

"Can't." Zeke squirmed and rubbed his chest. "It's down deep."

Ethan edged closer, anxious to see if Jayce understood.

"Tell Daddy what you mean."

Zeke bravely met his father's gaze. "M's-sorry."

"Sorry you were hurt?" Jayce checked.

"Uh-huh." With a blink, Zeke changed his mind. "Nuh-uh. Sorry cuz I was bad."

Jayce's expression cleared, and he hugged the boy. "Yes, you disobeyed … but I forgive you."

Zeke wiped his nose on his father's shirt. "That's all?"

"For now. Or was there something else you needed?"

Clinging close, Zeke mumbled, "D'ya still love me?"

"*Always.*"

READY TO GO

Jayce closed up shop during the county fair, but he still went in early to bake the apple turnovers they sold alongside kettle corn and caramel apples. He strolled down the front sidewalk with a spring in his step … oblivious to the Guardian perched on top of the family van. Opening the driver's side door, Jayce recalled the promise he'd made the previous evening.

"Can I help?"

"I leave early, buddy. You'll be sleeping."

"But if I'm ready?"

"Sure, sure."

And so Zeke had camped out overnight in the passenger seat.

Chuckling, Jayce backtracked to leave Naomi a note.

184
BIGGER IS BETTER

Tad kept a firm hold on his brother's hand but let Zeke lead the way. "That one!"

"Sorry, Zeke. You need to be taller before you can ride the big coasters."

"How high?"

Tad showed him the measuring stick. Even on tip-toe, Zeke couldn't make the mark. His big brother crouched and said, "Hey, be glad you're a Pomeroy. We're mostly tall, so you've got a head start on other four-year-olds."

Zeke straightened. "'Course I'm glad! Else, who'd be Jude's big brother?"

"Yep, you're a good'un."

As the pair headed for the merry-go-round, Ethan murmured, "As are you, Tad Pomeroy."

Grandpa Pete took a break from kettle corn to stroll around the fairgrounds. Zeke tagged along, hanging onto his grandfather's hand and chattering nonstop. Ethan was amused that the boy seemed to think he'd discovered this place. Pete had been coming to this fair since *he* was a boy.

"Are you hungry?" the old man asked.

"Yep!"

"Didn't you eat already?"

"Yep!"

"What did you have?"

Zeke cheerfully answered, "Funnel cake, corn dog, caramel apple, pretzel!"

"And you're *hungry* after all that?"

"Yep!"

"For what?"

Minutes later, they sat side-by-side on a bench, each manhandling an enormous smoked turkey drumstick.

186
OPEN SEATS

While Jayce and the boys piled into an oversized teacup, Ethan nudged Lucan. "Is it safe?"

The silver-eyed warrior chuckled. "Rest assured, Zeke will survive this tradition."

"Not *rest*. Ride!" exclaimed Jomei, grabbing Conrad and Ethan. "Open seats are fair game."

"Will we fit?" Ethan asked.

"Perks of being petite."

Juggling weapons. Bumping knees. And suddenly, the world blurred. Ethan had a hard time keeping track of Zeke amidst the whirl, but he could hear the boy's laughter mingling with that of his father and brothers.

Conrad smirked; he and Jomei grabbed the handle. Together, they sent their teacup spinning.

From his perch on Jayce's shoulders, Zeke grinned down at Jude, who rode on Naomi's. Ethan couldn't get close, but Alpheus stood right at the edge of the crowds. Spiraling lower, the pink-winged angel called, "May I?"

Alpheus understood in an instant and waved him down. Ethan landed on broad shoulders, straddling them just like the youngsters. Those Guardians nearest chuckled or complimented them on their ingenuity.

Ethan smiled fondly as Zeke held out his hand, touching fingertips with his little brother. "Get ready, Jude. It's gonna be … *boom*!"

Then fireworks exploded, and they sent off summer with smiles.

188
FREE RANGE

Naomi knelt in the garden, pulling carrots while keeping half an eye on Zeke. The boy ran in circles, trying to round up chickens. His mother mused, "Not keeping up, never catching up—I'm sure there's a lesson in there somewhere."

"Not giving up," Lucan said. "Because you are Faithful."

"Never far away," Ethan added. "Because you love him."

"She cannot hear you," reminded Alpheus. Jude sat under a bean tower beside a hen, cooing softly as he tried to feed her grass.

Naomi laughed quietly. "Let's go with … never a dull moment."

"Amen and amen," chorused three angels.

"**C**an I go outside?"

"Stay put," Naomi replied.

Ethan sat against the wall in the corner, a picture of patience compared to his jiggling, jouncing charge. Zeke finally asked, "Am I in trouble?"

"No." Naomi had pulled out every stitch of clothing in Zeke's drawers and was now ransacking storage tubs of hand-me-downs. "It's no use," she sighed. "Mud. Grass. Paint. Ink. Frayed cuffs. Missing belt loops. Torn knees."

He squirmed and protested, "My church clothes stay nice."

"Yes, but you need something *in between* church clothes and play clothes."

Zeke's face scrunched in puzzlement. "Whassat?"

Naomi smiled. "School clothes."

190
RUNNING OUT OF EXCUSES

"I dunno 'bout this, Momma." Zeke had been dragging his feet all morning. It was his first day of preschool. "Grandpa needs me!"

"Your chores will be waiting when you get home."

"And Jude's gonna miss me!" he argued.

"I'll keep him company."

Ethan's wings developed a twitch with each new excuse. Was preschool something to be feared?

"What about *you*, Momma?"

"I'll pick you up in time for lunch."

Zeke sulked.

In the parking lot, Naomi cheerfully exclaimed, "Oh, look! There's Jasper."

"Hey! Him and me are friends!" Zeke was off like a shot … and never looked back.

THIS ONE BEARS WATCHING

Ethan wanted to be inside the classroom with Zeke, but there were sixteen other Guardians in the rotation. He took his place to the south of the building without complaint.

An hour later, the Hedge's senior Guardian found him. "You're with Hezekiah Pomeroy?"

"Yes," Ethan replied, standing a little taller. "Zeke is under my watch-care."

The older warrior snorted. "Actually, he's under the table. Eating paste."

"I … apologize?"

"Inside, Ethan. I can see the writing on the wall. And it's in blue crayon."

"Did he …?"

"He did," the other Guardian confirmed. "To prove he knows the *whole* alphabet."

192
CLOG

Ethan picked up his booted feet and retreated into the hallway ahead of a wash of dirty water. It flowed along the wooden floor, then splashed down the back stairway. Beau spotted it first. "Momma, there's a flood!"

Naomi came running and found Zeke trying to use bath towels to dam the steady stream flowing from the toilet. "What did you do?" she gasped.

"Flushed," Zeke replied evasively.

"Flushed *what*?"

The boy scuffed at the floor with one toe, eyes downcast. Ethan turned his helpless gaze toward the ceiling. His young charge was certainly *inventive* when it came to play.

LEAFS

Ethan dreaded all the new avenues for mischief that preschool presented, but having teachers and classmates was bringing out interesting new facets to Zeke's personality.

"This paper says you only need *ten* leaves," Prissie said in bossy tones.

"I know," Zeke replied, adding sumac leaves to his collection.

"You have dozens!" his sister complained.

"I know," he repeated. "But what if people don't have as many trees as us. Or what if they only gots yellow leafs. This way, I can share!"

Prissie didn't look convinced, but Ethan was pleased … maybe even a little proud of Zeke's burgeoning generosity.

194
CAKE

Ethan couldn't fathom why he'd been Sent apart from Zeke.

"No lagging," Lucan chided as Jomei jostled the younger warrior along.

Zeke's preschool teacher exclaimed, "Thank you for coming in!"

"Is Zeke in trouble?" Jayce asked.

"Oh, no! This isn't *that* kind of parent-teacher moment. I only wanted to show you *this*." Four sheets of paper had been taped together to provide a canvas big enough for Zeke's craft project.

"Gracious!" Naomi murmured.

Neatly overlapping rows of leaves created an elaborate, three-tiered masterpiece. Jayce rubbed his chin, possibly to hide his grin.

Zeke's teacher bragged, "He's quiet the little artist!"

Tad tried to warn him. "Say, Zeke. About field trips …"

"Let him find out for himself!" protested Neil. "We all had to."

Ethan exchanged glances with Lucan, who smiled.

Zeke demanded, "Aren't field trips good?"

Neil tapped the permission slip. "Depends. Some places are great—fort, planetarium, zoo. And Momma packs an extra special lunch. No class for a day."

Zeke grinned. "That's good!"

"Not always," Neil said wisely. "The best stuff means a loooong drive."

Lucan leaned in to see what was on the printed sheet. "Ah."

"What?"

The big guardian said, "It will be a short drive."

196
Short Drive

Zeke was too busy talking to Jasper about zoos and forts to notice where he was. Ethan, who rode in an empty seat a few rows behind his charge, waved to Alpheus as the bus rolled to a stop in Orchard Lane's cul-de-sac.

When Zeke finally looked out a window, his expression blanked. Following his classmates down the aisle, he walked up to his teacher. "Am I in trouble?"

"Why would you think that?" she asked bemusedly.

He hopped off the bottom step and landed in his own driveway. Spreading his arms wide, he exclaimed, "'Cause you brought me home!"

Ethan found his charge's confusion understandable. This seemed to be some kind of Pomeroy rite of passage.

"Why are we at *my* house?" Zeke asked loudly.

"To learn about where apples come from."

"They grow on trees, Teacher. *Everyone* knows that!"

Grandpa Pete ambled over. "Something the matter, Zeke?"

"Uh-huh!" the four-year-old exclaimed. "I thought I was goin' on a trip to someone *else's* field!"

The old man chuckled. "Not everyone is lucky enough to have an orchard in their back yard. How 'bout we show your friends around some?"

Zeke perked up. "Sure! I know all the best places!"

PICK YOUR OWN

As two different Hedges merged into one around the Pomeroys' farm, Ethan flew low over the orchard, searching for a familiar mop of blond hair. The kids had been invited to pick their own apples, but Zeke seemed bent on showing Jasper their pigs. They were halfway to the back forty when a whisper caused Ethan's heart to lurch. *"Coddling, dawdling."*

"Blight!" he snapped, dropping to the ground.

Laughter hissed disconcertingly close. *"Questing, testing. Following, wallowing."*

Ethan whirled as his enemy slipped from the branches of a tree to stand barefoot in the grass. "You!"

Blight's lips quirked. "You called, friend?"

Keep it Secret, Keep it Safe

Ethan stared at Blight in disbelief. "How can you stand there so calmly?"

"Should I be distraught?"

Baffled that one of the Fallen would be so foolhardy, Ethan challenged, "Do you realize how many Guardians have been added to the Hedge this day?"

"Your concern is touching," the demon said with a smile. "Can you keep them at bay?"

Ethan opened his mouth, but slowly closed it. He'd never fight against his teammates, but neither could he raise the alarm. Was he actually aiding Blight?

"Sent to seek. Sent to find. Sent to me," the demon chanted in triumphant tones.

DENIAL

"I am Faithful; you are Fallen!"

Blight's blue eyes gleamed. "For now."

"Forever!" Ethan drew his sword. "I am *not* your friend!"

"When you teeter, I will push you. When you topple, I will catch you." The demon eased into the apple tree's shadow. "You will need a friend when grief takes you."

Ethan froze. "What do you mean?"

"I have watched, and I have waited. Patience has yielded a plan," boasted Blight as he blurred from view. Only his voice remained, as coy and confident as ever. *'I know what I want, and I know how to get it.'*

When Ethan returned from spending the wee hours on the farm's perimeter, Jomei met him on the roof. "Come and see!"

Even though Jayce's Guardian was all smiles, Ethan couldn't help asking, "Is Zeke in trouble?"

Jomei shook his head and hustled him into the master bedroom.

Lucan was waiting. "Ah. Look where your boy found shelter."

Zeke was sound asleep—hair mussed, cheeks flushed, mouth wide open. His hand was tucked safely into his mother's grasp, and his feet were jammed squarely into his father's stomach.

Three Guardians extended their wings over one little boy's refuge from bad dreams.

A Typical Wednesday

"**A**nything interesting happen today?" quizzed Raz, who was keeping Ethan company at the kitchen table.

The young warrior hesitated. "I am unsure."

"How can you *not* know?"

Ethan tried to explain. "Everything Zeke does interests me. However, I have noticed that most of the other Guardians are eager to see what he will do next."

"And what was today's *next*?"

Suddenly, Jayce's voice carried from the small office where he did his bookkeeping. "What …! Zeke, *what* is in your hair?"

"Glitters!"

Raz held his sides and laughed all the way through Zeke's rambling explanation of his latest craft-time mishap.

Angel Colors

Just before Christmas, the preschoolers made paper chains. Their tables were covered with strips of construction paper in every color, but before long, Ethan noticed that Zeke was only linking two—light pink and baby blue.

Jasper elbowed his friend. "How come those ones?"

"'Cause they're good angel colors!"

One of the other Guardians in the classroom nudged Ethan, saying, "I wonder what gave him *that* impression."

Could Zeke remember when Milo had bridged the gap? Or maybe a dream?

"Those are baby colors!" giggled one of the girls.

"Then I done good! 'Cause Jesus is a baby at Christmas!"

THE COOKS

Christmastime meant cookies, and Jayce let his little artist help out. In the bakery kitchen, Paul Cook stroked his bristling moustache. "That's a fine figure of a snowman, Zeke!"

"Yep!"

"You don't often see green ones," said the old man. Paul's wife Louise—or Auntie Lou, as she liked to be called—had recently come out of retirement to join the bakery staff. "Does he have elfish aspirations?"

"Grass stains," Zeke corrected. "From playing football."

"An inspired choice!"

Zeke grinned at Prissie, whose snowmen were white. "See? Uncle Lou says he's good!"

"Uncle *Who*?"

Mr. Cook laughed. "I'll be dubbed!"

When Othniel found Ethan lost in thought, he asked, "What troubles you, young warrior?"

"The Fallen."

"Understandable." The older Guardian took a seat beside him. "They trouble us all."

Ethan cautiously asked, "Have you ever met one of them?"

"Yes."

"Talked to him?"

"Yes," Othniel repeated, gazing at him from under bushy, red brows. "But swords are easier than words."

"We drive them off," Ethan said. "Is that enough?"

"For the day in which we stand, yes." Othniel frowned. "You have far eyes for one so new. May it make you wise for the time when such perspective is needed."

206
SUGAR COATED

Ethan was just as intrigued as his charge when the preschool teachers poured pastel rings onto the tables and passed out lengths of yarn on which to string them.

Zeke snatched, sniffed, and slipped one into his mouth. "Tastes good!"

"Who'd want cereal that tastes *bad*?" asked Jasper.

"Cereal," echoed the boy, trying another one. Being raised in a baker's household meant bread, muffins, and assorted pastries … not breakfast in a box.

Halfway through their craft time, Zeke's strand was the shortest. For every fruit-colored ring that made it onto his necklace, two found their way into his mouth.

Jayce leaned against the top bunk where Zeke sulked. "What's wrong, bud?"

"Valentine's."

"Sure, sure. Tomorrow's the big day."

"Yeah. 'Cept my present for Momma was too breakful."

"Breakable?"

"Broked," Zeke corrected, spreading his hands. "We throwed it away."

"What did you make?"

He mumbled, "My hand."

Rubbing his chin, Jayce ventured, "A handprint?"

"Uh-huh."

Ethan could see how disappointed Zeke was. Thankfully, the boy's father was just as perceptive. "How about we find *another* way to give Momma our love?"

The next day, Jayce served an elaborate torte, decorated with whipped cream, shaved chocolate, and one little boy's handprint.

208
Sense of Humor, Intact

Ethan couldn't resist inviting Garrick and Yannis to visit the preschool before the Valentine's Day decorations were taken down. "What is *that*?"

Chuckles rippled around the room as Ethan explained, "A cherub."

The two muscular archers traded a long look. Yannis protested, "*This* is what children are taught about cherubim?"

"At least he carries a bow," Garrick ventured.

Yannis shook his head. "But why are his arrows tipped with hearts?"

Before long, both Protectors were up on tiptoe, posing with their bows, and leading a song of celebration for the children, their Guardians, and the God who loved them all.

Ethan was afraid Zeke would be bored with his class's springtime gardening project. Not so.

"This is weird," he muttered to Jasper. "Seeds go in the ground. Not in eggs."

"I'll tell you what's weird," his best friend replied. "These eggs!"

"Nuh-uh. They're just regular ones. Momma and me brought them for teacher."

Jasper studied his soil-filled eggshell. "But this's green! And huge! Maybe they're *dinosaur* eggs!"

Zeke snorted. "Ain't you never heard of ducks?"

"Ain't you never heard of 'magination?"

By morning's end, the two boys had convinced their classmates that they were planting magic beans in dragon eggs.

210
CLOUDLESS

Ethan loved having Zeke under his watch-care, but too often, that meant all he could do was watch … and care. "Not the orchard," he sighed. Blight delighted in dropping in on Ethan whenever they were amidst the trees.

Suddenly, Zeke stopped and stared up through branches thick with blossoms. Snowy white flowers hung in fragrant clouds, dazzling against a cloudless blue sky. "Wow," he whispered, soft and sincere.

The single, worshipful note sent a tremor of joy through Ethan's wings, scattering the worries that had kept him from noticing nature's beauty.

He responded in kind. "Amen and amen."

Six children filed into their parents' bedroom, oldest to youngest, followed by Jayce, who presented his wife with a breakfast tray and a kiss atop her tousled head. "Happy Mother's Day," he greeted.

"I made pancakes!" Neil announced.

"I put on the blueberries," Prissie quickly added.

Beau said, "I made juice."

Tad helped arrange the pillows behind his mom's back before confiding, "The flowers are from me."

Naomi looked expectantly at her remaining sons, and Zeke exclaimed, "Guess what me and Jude did!"

When she turned a baffled look on her husband, Jayce cleared his throat. "You'll remember Valentine's Day …?"

212
Rainy Day Campers

Ethan sat on the floor in the family room, smiling as he watched over Zeke and Jude. Blankets and chairs made a tent, and a circle of building blocks represented their campfire. Both boys were draped in borrowed flannel shirts with the sleeves rolled up.

"Like this," Zeke repeated.

"Dis," echoed Jude.

"Almost. See here? You gotta fit it *through*."

His little brother giggled softly. "Dis?"

"Nope. Watch me," Zeke urged, untangling the boot laces again.

Ethan propped his chin on his hand and hummed happily. His young charge wasn't just looking forward to summer; he was preparing for it!

Remember When

For his fifth birthday, Jayce invited Zeke to help make his own cake.

"That looks familiar," Jomei remarked to Ethan as the man pinned a familiar craft project to the bakery kitchen's wall.

"You saved it!" Zeke exclaimed

His dad beamed. "Sure, sure. That's our inspiration!"

Father and son spent all morning making chocolate leaves, recreating the cake Zeke had designed, chatting all the while. "Was you there when I was borned?"

"Me and Momma both!"

"Was I little?"

Jayce held out his hands. "Just this big."

Jomei smiled nostalgically. "Jayce's prayers were sweet."

Ethan nodded. "As was your song."

A WIDER WORLD

Early the morning after Zeke graduated to a two-wheeler, Ethan jogged after his charge, who wobbled determinedly onto the gravel road.

"Wow. Dad was right," Tad remarked from his seat on the fence. "Where are you going, Zeke?"

"Work."

His oldest brother shook his head. "You're not allowed to ride down Orchard Lane without a buddy, and you're not allowed on the highway. Period."

Zeke pouted. "But …!"

Tad patiently asked, "How far could you go on the trike?"

"The driveway."

"And what's your range *now*?"

Ethan breathed a sigh of relief when Tad graciously agreed to be Zeke's buddy.

215
WHITE NOISE

A fan droned steadily. Shades were drawn against the sun's glare. Other than the *buzz-thump* of a fat fly searching for a way out, the house was quiet. Even Zeke. Ethan's charge lay on the floor in front of the fan, his flushed face tilted into the stream of air cooling his sticky skin. Peaceful enough on the surface, but his Guardian knew better.

As Zeke poked with one finger, testing to see how close he could get to whirling fan blades, Ethan groaned, "Does he even *think* about repercussions?"

Conrad simply smirked and gave the fan's cord another jiggle.

PUT ME DOWN

Along one side of the church foyer, a table with sign-up sheets awaited volunteers, and Zeke was standing on tiptoe, carefully adding his name to one of the lists. Ethan checked to see if the boy's 'Z' was forward or backward this time.

Jayce ambled over. "What's this?"

"I can write my name!" his son boasted.

"These are only for volunteers."

"I know."

Jayce rubbed his chin. "It's not a game. This is for a church work day."

Zeke nodded. "I know. I can help!"

"Fair enough." Without another word, Jayce added his name under his son's on the list.

Church Work Day

There was a lengthy list of jobs to do—clearing out gutters, trimming hedges, and painting a classroom. However, as eager as Zeke and Jasper were to clamber up ladders and dip into paint cans, Jayce needed something more suited to five-year-olds.

Rescue arrived in the form of Uncle Lou. The old man stroked his moustache. "Jayce, could you possibly recommend two men of valor—stout hearts, straight backs, stiff upper lips? I've been given a *perilous* task!"

Ethan spent the rest of the day perching on pews while his charge crawled underneath, looking for wads of gum to dislodge.

218
No Horseplay

From the end of the high dive board, Ethan watched his charge fidget and squirm while a teacher outlined the rules of the pool. It was the first day of swimming lessons, and Zeke was eager to get into the water. But before he could learn what to *do*, there was a long list of *don'ts*.

Zeke elbowed the freckled boy next to him, whispering, "Can you swim?"

"Nope."

"Me either," Zeke admitted. "But if I learn, I can try *that*."

The other boy looked straight at Ethan, who blinked in surprise, then chuckled. Zeke's goals always were *lofty*.

Two Techniques, One Result

Ethan and Zeke both watched in solemn fascination as the freckled boy, whose name turned out to be Timothy, took the time to stuff his spiky brown hair under a swimming cap. Goggles came next. Then a nose plug. Finally, the five-year-old eased into the pool one cautious step at a time, gripping the edge the whole way.

"Aren't ya coming?" asked Zeke's new friend.

"Ready or not! Here I come!"

Ethan smiled at way the freckle-faced boy ducked and covered as Zeke charged to the edge and launched right over Timothy's head, entering the pool with a mighty splash.

SUMMER FRIEND

The blond boy in red trunks and the freckled boy in the blue swimming cap were easy to spot, chugging along side-by-side on their boogie boards.

"I did so dive!" Zeke exclaimed. "Off the top step!"

With a funny little snicker, Timothy replied, "You *flopped*."

Zeke grinned. "Well, my splashes are biggest!"

"Prove it!" challenged his friend, kicking harder.

Ethan smiled as the boys churned across the shallow end. Zeke's courage was rubbing off on Timothy, and in exchange, Timothy made sure Zeke looked before he leapt. It was a good combination, and Ethan wished it could have lasted longer.

TEST OF COURAGE

On the last day of swimming lessons, Zeke finally received permission to climb the big ladder. Timothy couldn't be persuaded to join his friend, but he waited on his boogie board, right next to their swimming teacher. She called, "Ready when you are, Zeke!"

"Almost!"

Ethan was waiting for his charge at the top of the ladder, so he saw Zeke's eyes widen and knees wobble. "High," the boy whispered.

"We have flown higher, in dreams," Ethan whispered.

"Gonna chicken out?" hollered Neil, who stood with the other Pomeroys. Momma's camera was ready.

"You watch!" Zeke challenged. "I'm gonna *fly*!"

Summer Reading Program

Zeke propped his chin on the counter and stared up at the librarian. "Is it time?"

"Ten more minutes," she replied, her usual bright smile a little forced.

Blue eyes drifted to the wall clock that ticked away the seconds. "Now?" he asked.

"That was ten seconds, Zeke."

"Oh."

Ethan huffed in amusement when his charge tried to pass the time by holding his breath.

After turning red and gasping noisily, Zeke asked, "Is it time *yet*?"

Naomi collared her son. "Sorry! He's *very* excited for the magic show."

With a wan smile, the woman simply said, "Eight more minutes."

ENJOY THE JOURNEY

"**I** can't believe we're already here," murmured Naomi. "I'm not sure I'm ready for this."

Jayce chuckled. "I'm not sure his teacher's ready for this. But Zeke is."

His wife smiled. "I wonder if *this* is what they mean when they say someone's born ready."

Alpheus tapped Ethan's shoulder. "Are *you* ready?"

"Always and never," he admitted with a wry smile. "I cannot say for certain."

"I don't hear nothing." Zeke's red sneakers did a dance of impatience on the gravel.

Jayce asked, "In a rush, son?"

"'Course!"

"To get to school?"

Zeke blinked. "Nuh-uh. I wanna ride the *bus*!"

224
A CORD OF THREE STRANDS

Ethan helped escort a line of five-year-olds to their classroom. Once Zeke was through the door, he caught sight of his best friend from church. "Jasper! You came to school?"

"Grandmama says I gotta."

"Me, too," Zeke sighed. "Dad said to learn lotsa stuff. And not eat paste."

"You're here!"

Ethan was smiling as broadly as his charge when Zeke turned and goggled at a familiar freckled face. Flapping his arms excitedly, he hollered, "Hey, I know you! Timothy!"

By the time the teacher settled everyone down enough to start class, Zeke, Jasper, and Timothy had decided to be inseparable.

ROUGH AND TUMBLE

Five-year-olds looked harder to pin down than a flock of yahavim, yet by snack time, the kindergarten teacher knew who could read, who needed reminders to use the bathroom, and who would be her troublemakers. "Zeke, return to your seat."

"Don't have one!"

"Your name is right here."

"Nuh-uh. My name's Zeke."

"This is your *full* name," his teacher gently corrected.

Jasper leaned over. "Full?"

Timothy squeezed closer. "What's it say?"

Ethan's charge slapped his hands over the name tag. "It's supposed to be spelled *Zeke* … only 'cept Teacher wrote it wrong. So I'm gonna sit with the gerbils."

Farmer's Almanac

Zeke didn't like chairs. "I can hear you fine from here, Teacher," he promised from inside the block fortress he'd been building.

She hesitated. "Can you tell me about our lesson?"

"Almanac stuff."

"Excuse me?"

Ethan felt a small burst of pride when, Zeke replied, "Spring's for planting. Summer's for weeding. Autumn's for apples. And I already know 'bout weeks and days. Tuesdays are best 'cause of storytime. Are you gonna do storytime again? That part's good."

"Yes, Zeke. That's the very next thing. Will you be listening?"

With a wave, he repeated, "I can hear you fine from here!"

SHAVE AND A HAIRCUT

When Grandpa Pete headed into town for a haircut, he invited Zeke along. Ethan looked on with the old guys swapping gossip and sections of newspaper while the barber trimmed his charge's hair.

Once he finished up, Zeke said, "Shave, please!"

All conversation stopped.

Long glances over reading glasses were traded.

Grandpa Pete asked, "What's that cost, Gus?"

"Oh, I reckon it's still two bits."

"Guess I can spare a quarter. Set him up."

Zeke sat tall in the chair, unaware that he was taking part in a longstanding boyhood ritual … and that Gus wasn't actually using a blade.

228
GOOD SPORT

Ethan dropped from a tree limb as Zeke plunged into the overgrown grass along the yard's edge. "I got it!" the boy shouted.

"Hurry up!" called Neil.

Tad waved broadly. "More to the left, Zeke!"

"I know!"

Football season was in full swing, and Neil used all his spare time for practice. He let his kid brother join in, so long as Zeke chased down overthrown passes. Ethan did what he could to help, gently lifting aside the worst of the brambles, steering clear of sticker bushes, and nudging the football out from behind a stump.

Zeke hollered, "Found it!"

WEEKEND GETAWAY

On Saturday morning, Naomi did a double-take. "Zeke?"

As the boy skidded to a stop, Ethan breathed, "Finally."

Lucan chuckled. "She has always been quick to notice small things."

Naomi scrutinized her son. "What's in your pocket, Zeke?" she asked lightly.

"School stuff."

"What *kind* of school stuff?"

Zeke's zipped-up coat pocket jumped, and he quickly cupped it with his hand. "Y'know how Grandpa says you gotta take care of your animals every day, no skipping?"

Naomi rephrased her question. "*Who's* in your pocket, Zeke?"

"Zippity …."

"You brought home a *gerbil*?"

Zeke held up two fingers. "… and Doo-Dah."

CONTRABAND

Ethan could understand his charge's fascination. The boy's father ran a bakery, and his grandmother kept their cookie jar stocked with homemade goodies. So when Jasper brought out a pre-packaged snack in a crinkling cellophane wrapper, Zeke asked, "Whassat?"

"Zert," his friend replied.

That evening, Jayce Pomeroy drove Zeke to a convenience store outside Harper where they wouldn't be recognized. Side-by-side in the front seat of the van, they bit into golden sponge cakes.

Ethan chuckled when the boy's face screwed up in confusion. Jayce's expression was almost as funny. Especially when Zeke looked for a place to spit.

"*Yuck.*"

Resemblances

Alpheus beckoned to Ethan, who stole up in time to overhear Jude ask, "How come we're brothers?"

Zeke answered, "Dad and mom."

"But we don't *look* like brothers." Zeke's blond mop and blue eyes bore little resemblance to Jude's fine, dark hair and gray eyes.

"You look like Tad."

Jude wibbled. "But I wanna look like *you*."

Taking off his plaid coat, Zeke buttoned it onto the three-year-old. "There!" he said. "This coat usta be mine when I was little like you. It's a hand-me-down from your brother. And that's me. See?"

The little boy hugged himself and smiled. Satisfied.

232
Applesauce Doughnuts

On a rainy Saturday in early October, Zeke lost his usual job. Customers weren't interested in picking their own apples in this weather, so he and Tad hung out in the barn. Ethan could tell Zeke was bored, which usually led to trouble.

"Daddy shoulda let me go to the bakery," the boy grumbled.

Ethan blessed Naomi for choosing that moment to intervene. "Zeke, can you help?"

He ran to his mother, who asked him to put applesauce doughnuts into bags whenever there was an order.

"Just like Daddy!" he exclaimed.

Naomi laughed softly. "More than he likes to admit!"

Sticky strands. Gooey chunks. Zeke held out two hands full of pumpkin guts. "It's squishy!"

Prissie rolled her eyes. "Keep scraping." She and Beau sorted through the orange glop, rescuing seeds to toast.

Zeke wrinkled his nose but dug back in. Ethan was close enough to hear him mumble, "Don't need no sister to tell me what's fun." Up to his armpits in the biggest pick from their patch, Zeke cleaned it out the way Tad had shown him.

Ethan saw inspiration strike and groaned. Alpheus's deep laugh soon joined his chuckle as Zeke helped Jude climb *inside* the pumpkin.

234
THINK OF THE CHILDREN

Heavy rains dragged the last of the leaves from the trees. It was too wet to work or play outside, which left Zeke restless and ready to roughhouse. Neil wasn't much better off. "Please? You're better at knots than me!"

Tad stared up into the barn rafters. "Kind of a hassle, getting out the big ladder."

Neil waved at Zeke and Jude. "Think of the children!"

Ethan joined the brothers' Guardians on the wide beam where Tad leaned the ladder and secured his knots. Then the Pomeroy boys proved that rainy days, rafters, and rope swings were a perfect combination.

TRUCKLOADS AND GALAXIES

"**M**y 'Lo! Teach me something good!"

Milo chuckled. "What do you want to learn, my 'Eke?"

"Something *big*!"

Ethan smiled sheepishly at the Messenger, who winked his way before asking, "How many apples did you harvest this year?"

"Dunno. Lots."

"How many stars are in the sky each night?"

"Too many to count?"

"For anyone?" prompted Milo.

Zeke's face scrunched up. "God might know."

"Yep. He knows them all. So! How many people does God love?"

"Truckloads and galaxies?"

"That's right," Milo replied. "Yet He knows every single one. Including *you*."

Zeke's whole countenance brightened. "That's good. I like that."

236
SEE FOR YOURSELF

"Is it sticky?"

"Very," his father replied. "And also very hot. That's why we keep that ice water close."

"Oh yeah?"

Ethan found Zeke's approach to life baffling. Even when he was told the truth in the simplest possible terms, he didn't always accept the facts. The boy wanted to taste for himself, see for himself, know for himself. Oftentimes, that meant learning the hard way, but Ethan was beginning to think that this wasn't necessarily bad. When Zeke grasped something, he understood it all the way down to his toes.

"Careful, Zeke!" Jayce exclaimed.

Ice water splashed. "Yep. Hot."

Thy Word Have I Hid

At the sound of tearing paper, Prissie gasped, "Zeke! What are you *doing*!"

Ethan glanced sheepishly at his mentor, whose black eyes glinted. "I'm curious, too."

Zeke held up a page from his Bible. "This."

"That's terrible!"

Zeke frowned. "Nuh-uh. It's not a library book."

"But why …?"

"To keep it with me." Carefully folding the page, he explained, "Milo said."

"Milo *couldn't* have told you to rip up your Bible."

Stuffing it inside his shirt, Zeke explained, "He said to hide it next to my heart."

Prissie groaned. Ethan covered his eyes. Conrad smirked and said, "Close. Very close."

238
SHARED BLAME

"Jude started it," Ethan accused, his tone light.

Alpheus couldn't deny it, but he rushed to his charge's defense. "Accidentally."

"His aim was *accidentally* excellent." Ducking, Ethan added, "And Beau's has improved considerably."

"Zeke was too quick to retaliate." Alpheus leaned to one side, evading Neil's volley.

Ethan nodded. "And the others should not have followed suit, but even Tad …!" Ten minutes ago, he wouldn't have guessed that slices of warm pumpkin pie and spoons were the ingredients for a full-scale food fight.

Moments later, Lucan arrived. Taking in the spattered kitchen and splattered brothers, he responded predictably. "Ah."

LADIES FIRST

Zeke was good at the games they played in class, but musical chairs were his undoing. Both his father and grandfather expected the Pomeroy boys to behave as gentlemen. Ethan smiled as the boy tried to reconcile his competitive streak with basic courtesies.

The music stopped. There was a mad scramble for chairs. And Zeke hesitated. Which was all the opening little Meredith needed to claim the last seat.

When Zeke sat on the sidelines, Timothy whispered, "You were closer."

"Yep."

Jasper demanded, "Why'd you let her win?"

Zeke grumbled, "I gotta ask Daddy if manners change for musical chairs."

TO EACH THEIR OWN

Ethan sat at the far end of the kitchen table, where Zeke and Jude were engaged in a silly game of Thanksgiving one-upmanship. The three-year-old chose, "Momma."

His older brother countered with, "Daddy."

Prissie rolled her eyes. "We're *all* thankful for them. Obviously."

"Chickens," said Jude.

Zeke's glare dared Prissie to argue. "Brothers."

With a shy look, Jude offered, "Sister."

Prissie's expression softened, and she stopped meddling.

Her Guardian chuckled, and when Ethan caught Tamaes's eye, the older warrior joined the game. "Prissie."

Alpheus's deep voice quickly answered, "Jude."

Laughing, Ethan offered his first, best reason to give thanks. "Zeke."

TRIAL AND ERROR

Ethan looked on with apprehension the day his charge decided to try lying. It was all very deliberate … like an experiment Zeke was running.

"He does not flee from evil," Ethan murmured.

"He prods it to see what it'll do." There was an odd resignation in Conrad's gaze. "Then makes up his mind accordingly."

Up until now, Zeke had been truthful; this newest ploy spelled disaster. Ethan's wings wilted. "He has no idea how fragile trust can be."

"He'll learn."

"Why must it always be the hard way?"

Conrad shook his head. "At least he *learns*. Some never do."

Broken Trust

Zeke started small. A little fib here. An evasive answer there. Ethan watched the boy play with lies as if they were toys.

Several gingerbread men were found beheaded. A broken ornament turned up under sofa cushions. Odd jobs were left unfinished. And nobody seemed to realize what Zeke was up to. Except perhaps Naomi. Although her tone remained casual, her questions grew more pointed. "Who left these peelings on the floor?"

"It wasn't me," Zeke quickly replied.

"Is this … *jam*?"

"It wasn't me."

Ethan cringed when Naomi remarked, "Someone didn't eat their vegetables."

Zeke repeated, "It wasn't me."

SIN AND SORROW

Mother, brothers, sister—Zeke's careless lies piled up. But when the boy lied to his father, Ethan knew something was different. "That cost him."

"It cut him," Jomei corrected.

That night, Ethan held his breath as he stepped into dreams. Zeke stared hard, as if trying to place an almost-familiar face. His Guardian knelt and asked, "Why are you sad?"

"I did something bad," Zeke confessed. "It *was* me."

"I know. I saw." The boy barreled into him, clinging tightly to the truth. Ethan folded his arms and wings around him. "What will you do?"

"Fess up. All the way."

Private Conversation

The next day, Zeke tugged Jayce's sleeve and grimly asked to talk. Father and son bundled up and headed for the barns, a sure sign that this was serious.

Two angels trailed after. "Jayce looks heartbroken," Ethan whispered.

Jomei nodded. "Because he *is*."

"So is Zeke."

Compassion filled the older warrior's green eyes. "Maybe so, but all Jayce knows is that his son has strayed."

Ethan pressed his hand over his breastplate. "I do not care for this suspense."

Jomei's eyebrows arched. "You feel it, too? Good. It's not just me."

"Feel … what?"

Hurrying Ethan along, Jomei replied, "Anticipation!"

LUMPS OF COAL

"You wanted to say something?" Jayce prompted, dropping to a seat on the hay bales.

"Yep." Zeke plopped down next to his father. Pressing both hands over his stomach, he solemnly announced, "I know why there's lumps of coal in bad boys' stockings. Feels heavy."

"Is this …?" Jayce sighed. "Are you worried about disappointing Santa Claus?"

Ethan glanced up as Conrad strode in, quickly followed by Lucan. But most of his attention was on Zeke, who looked startled. "He's only here once at Christmas. *You're* my daddy."

Jayce smiled weakly. "All the time. Even when I'm not sure how."

246
Cloud of Witnesses

Zeke launched into a winding confession of his wrongdoings, but Ethan was distracted by the stirring of more arrivals. A scan of the barn rafters confirmed that all of Tycho's Flight were there, and the rest of the Hedge was assembling. "What …?" Ethan murmured.

Conrad's hand locked on his bicep. *"This,"* his mentor replied, calling his attention back to Zeke.

The boy was the picture of exasperation. "I *know* how this works, Daddy. I been paying 'tention!"

Ethan's breath caught. "Th-this is what he meant when he said he wanted to fess up?"

"This," Conrad repeated, his eyes shining.

ON THEIR KNEES

Jayce knelt down in front of his son. "Sure, sure. Tell me how it works, Zeke."

While the boy proved he had indeed been paying attention, Ethan bit his trembling lip, then sank to the floor. The terrible game of lies would end in grace? Amazing.

The growing crowd of angels parted to let someone through. Milo fell to his knees beside Ethan.

Milo's hair was wild, and his breath came in tight bursts. "This boy … makes me … race." Tears spilled down the Messenger's cheeks as he pressed his hand over his heart. "Looks like he *always* will."

248
Unwavering Gaze

Conrad dropped to one knee at Ethan's other side. Mentor and apprentice silently bore witness to Zeke's profession of faith. As Jayce and Zeke prayed together, it became hard to breathe. The young Guardian hadn't known that joy could be so intense, it would pierce him straight through.

Every part of Ethan was shaking … except his gaze. Unwavering, he watched eternity embrace his charge.

On the day Hezekiah Pomeroy was born, Ethan had been overwhelmed by the rush of confused emotions. As Zeke was born again, Ethan was equally overwhelmed, but this time by clarity.

Awed, he whispered, *"Beautiful."*

 ROUGH AND TUMBLE

Counted Among the Beloved

There was no need to assemble for evensong. The heavenly chorus still swelled with angels rejoicing over Zeke's faith. Once the boy was tucked in for the night, the other Hedge members gradually drifted back to their posts until only Conrad and Ethan stood at the foot of the bunk bed, singing in tightly-woven harmonies.

Finally, even his mentor fell silent, and Ethan offered one last song, a lilting lullaby overflowing with love and joy.

Drifting in that place between waking and sleeping, Zeke turned onto his side and tucked his hand under his cheek. Smiling faintly, he mumbled, "Byoot-ful."

250
MENDED

As they watched Zeke sleep, Ethan whispered, "Does this change things for you?"

Conrad searched his face. "In what sense?"

Ethan tentatively touched his own ear.

Expression clearing, Conrad remarked, "You never once asked how I came to be pierced."

"I meant to. Eventually."

"*Ask*, Ethan. You can benefit from my sorrow, just as I've benefited from your joy."

Ducking his head, he shyly asked, "Who was your charge?"

"A quiet, careful boy. He never gave me trouble, yet he wounded me deeply." Conrad's lips quirked. "But God knew what I needed to mend."

"Zeke?"

Conrad replied, "No, Ethan. *You*."

In the afterglow of joy surrounding his young charge's salvation, Ethan let his guard slip. "Have you seen Zeke?" he called to Othniel, who stood on the farmhouse's roof.

The red-maned warrior pointed, and an ominous *creak* sounded from that direction.

Ethan sprinted for the machine shed, bursting through the door in time to throw his weight against the teetering shelves Zeke was climbing. The boy dropped to the floor and slowly backed away, and Ethan let his forehead *thunk* against the unit.

He had expected the life-changing decision to be more … life-changing. Yet somehow Zeke was still Zeke.

252
AN ILL WIND

During a January thaw, Ethan caught a familiar whisper that chilled his heart. *"There, your care is cared for. Now live carefree, like me."*

Following Blight's hissing laughter into the shadows behind the machine shed, Ethan quietly called, "What do you mean?"

"A boy deemed redeemable. A guard seems unseemly." The demon slunk out from behind a tree and smiled. "I was patient. See? I am rewarded."

A demon rejoicing over a child's salvation? Impossible. Ethan gripped his sword more tightly. "What exactly were you waiting for?"

Blight's blue eyes glittered. "Freed from obligation. Free to oblige me ... *friend*."

One Last Obstacle

Ethan didn't like the direction Blight seemed to be taking. "I am *not* your friend, and I am not freed from my responsibilities." Leveling his sword at the demon, he swore, "So long as Zeke is alive, I will …."

Blight's eyebrows lifted. "You see? Simplicity."

"No." Ethan took a step closer. "I will *not* …!"

Again, Blight interrupted. "Fuss and fester if you must. But bid farewell. He goes to God. You come with me."

Ethan was staggered. "You expect me to join you after threatening my charge?"

"I expect you to flail … and fail … and Fall."

254
Interference

The demon smiled as he spoke of abominable things. Ethan was horrified, even a little frightened, but he stood firm. "You cannot touch him."

"Neither can you," Blight murmured.

Ethan blinked. That wasn't entirely true. Under certain circumstances, he was able to get close to Zeke. But by the same token, couldn't a clever demon interfere in someone's life? Get close?

When Ethan blinked again, his tormentor was nodding. "You *do* understand! We understand one another." Blight's conviction made it sound like he knew what he was talking about. "Can't you see? You and me. We are meant to be!"

Ethan felt oddly alone, and his songs suffered. Concentrating on anything was tough. "Unlike Zeke."

Solving a puzzle. Building a tower. Shoveling the porch. If the boy began a task, he followed it through to the end. "Is resolve enough?"

He was still shaking his head when his view of Zeke was swathed in green. "Guess who?"

When Raz lowered his wings, there stood Verrill, arms open. The young Guardian was so very relieved to see his confidants that he pulled the slender Messenger into a fierce hug.

Resolve was good. Friends were better. And God would receive Ethan's best.

256
POTLUCK SUNDAY

Ethan slipped into the fellowship hall in time to see Zeke corner Milo. "Can I sit with you, my 'Lo?"

"If your parents don't mind, my 'Eke."

Halfway through lunch, Zeke got down to business. "Can I come to your class now?"

"Why would you skip grades?"

"On account of I'm a Christian."

Milo wrapped his arm around the boy's shoulders. "I'm *glad*."

Zeke scrutinized his face. "That's what everyone says, but you mean it most. How come?"

Cutting a glance Ethan's way, Milo repeated a message he'd delivered once before. "Do you have *any* idea how much you're loved?"

Loading Questions

"**D**oes that mean *yes*?" demanded Zeke, a spoonful of mashed potatoes halfway to his mouth.

"No," Milo replied with gentle firmness. "You'll move up to my class when the time's right."

"Two years, plus a half."

The mailman smiled. "Have you been counting down?"

"My whole life!"

Ethan chuckled.

"Meanwhile, you know where to find me. Not everything you learn about God comes from Sunday school."

Zeke chewed on that … and his potato roll. "I can ask questions?"

"Any time."

"I got one." All seriousness, the boy asked, "According to God, is a secret the same as a lie?"

258
COME AND SEE

Ethan wondered how Milo would answer, since the mailman carried an amazing secret of his own. But the Messenger seemed more interested in finding out what was behind Zeke's question. "Do you have a secret that's worrying you?"

"Yep."

"Is it something you can tell me about?"

The boy glanced around the crowded room. "I'd mostly rather not. But since it's you … I could *show* you."

Milo's expression shifted, and Ethan was sure it was a Sending. "Sure, Zeke. Where and when?"

"Can you come over after church?"

He offered a reprise. "If your parents don't mind, my 'Eke."

AFTERNOON TROMP

While Milo strapped on a pair of snowshoes, he sought Ethan's gaze and silently remarked, *"I sincerely doubt Zeke is harboring any dark secrets. But you look worried. Anything I should know?"*

Ethan could only promise, "I will be with you."

Zeke stomped in a circle, testing his own footgear. "Let's go!"

Once the pair turned past the chicken coop and headed into the orchard, Ethan was sure. Zeke was taking Milo to his secret place, the special tree where he spent his free time plotting new mischief. It was also one of the spots where Blight loved to loiter.

COVER YOUR TRACKS

"Won't our tracks give away your hiding place?"

Zeke grinned. "I thought of that. This is the wrong way."

Milo chuckled. "Not bad."

"Who decides if something is bad … or if it's good?" asked Zeke. "Because Prissie thinks muddy footprints is *bad*, even if I got the mud from doing what Grandpa called *good* work."

"By any chance, does your mother have a rule about taking off your shoes before going inside?"

Ethan smiled at Zeke's sheepish nod.

Milo said, "Then you just gave an excellent example of how doing good work won't cancel out the messes we make."

Milo tromped along, giving his full attention to Zeke. "Is this the scenic route, or are we lost?"

Zeke's eyes rolled. "How could I get lost at home?"

"Then I'll place my trust in you."

The Messenger's casual reminder deepened Ethan's resolve. Weren't these lessons they'd learned together? Trust your teammates. Trust God.

Moments later, a swish of purple caught his eye. High overhead, two cherubim spiraled, their aerial dance accompanied by a carefree song of praise. Yannis and Garrick spotted him and swung low. Arm raised in greeting, Ethan murmured, "Thanks be to God, who knows our every need."

A Tree for All Seasons

Zeke's mitten thumped against bark. "This is my special tree."

Milo contemplated the apple tree. "You found the perfect hiding place, right in the middle of a bunch of ordinary trees."

The boy was beaming as he clambered up to his favorite seat. "This is where I like to sit."

"I see. And what do you do out here, all by yourself?"

"Mostly depends on my tree," Zeke said seriously. "If it's blossom time, I watch the honeybees. If it's summertime, I watch light between the leaves. If it's harvesttime, I eat apples."

"Is that all?"

Zeke shrugged. "I think."

Countable

Hooking his elbows over another branch, Milo asked, "Why would you be worried about a secret like this?"

"I heard Daddy talking about being countable," Zeke explained. "So I been thinking. If I gotta be countable for my secrets, my 'Lo is best."

Garrick elbowed Ethan. "Your charge is almost as cute as you."

"Uh. Dorable," agreed Yannis. "But asking an *angel* to keep you accountable? He has no idea what he's in for."

Milo favored them with a wink.

Ethan couldn't bring himself to join in on their laughter. Not when the wind carried hints of Blight's hissing amusement.

264
Unguarded Moment

The archers flew off while Milo and Zeke retreated to the porch steps to remove their snowshoes.

Stomp, tromp. Worry, flurry. The sing-song voice gained strength as its owner stepped into view. "Blight in the yard; double the guard?" he asked sweetly.

"They were only visiting." Ethan glanced away to make certain Zeke was safely inside. When he looked back, he was inches from a pair of bright blue eyes.

At his gasp, Blight smiled benignly and whispered, "*Boo.*"

Before Ethan could gather his wits, the demon was gone, taking a goodly portion of the young warrior's confidence with him.

"**Y**ou should come skating. Can you?" Zeke asked.

Jasper countered, "Visit? Or skate?"

Zeke said, "Both. 'Cause I have a pond. What about you, Timothy?"

"Never tried. Is it hard?"

"*Easy*!" Zeke took a running start at the slick pavement and skidded several feet. "See?"

For the rest of recess, the three friends careened around, laughing and cheering one another on.

From his perch on the school roof, Ethan pondered God's reasons for sending a single Guardian after Blight. Was it because one angel was enough to stop him? Or because only an angel who was alone could catch him?

266
After Evensong

Ethan felt the familiar brush of Conrad's wings as his mentor joined him beside Zeke's bed.

Hours passed in simple silence, but near sunrise, Conrad said, "I *know* something's troubling you." At Ethan's startled look, the swordsman smirked. "Don't underestimate mentors. We're as perceptive as mothers."

"I … cannot explain."

"No matter. I see God's hand in this." Conrad confided, "Your songs reveal new depths. A maturity of perspective."

Ethan couldn't hide his bewilderment.

"We can't always see our own progress," Conrad continued. "Maybe that's why we serve in pairs. We *need* one another's perspective. And now you know mine."

Ice Folly

Faith threaded through Ethan's heart like a song, leaving no room for worries or doubts. Blight's threat definitely kept him on guard, but nothing could diminish his trust. Or the delight Zeke brought to his days. Ethan sat with a few other angels on the rail of the red bridge overlooking the Pomeroys' pond.

"Faster!" challenged Zeke.

Jasper grinned. "I'll catch you!"

"No fair!" complained Timothy. "You could already skate!"

"You're doing good," Zeke replied, spreading his arms wide. "It's like flying."

The freckle-faced boy grumbled, "People can't fly."

"Can too." Zeke's eyes took on a faraway look. "In dreams."

CHEF COAT

Zeke hung on his Dad's arm and pointed at the computer screen. "That one! Just like yours!"

"Looks good." With a sidelong glance, Jayce said, "You know, your birthday's just around the corner."

"But I want it *now*." Zeke wheedled, "I have money."

"How much have you saved?"

"A whole piggy bank full!"

"Bring it down, and we'll see if there's enough."

Ethan slid into one of the chairs and propped his chin on his hand. This was going to be interesting.

With a rattle, Zeke shook out his riches onto the kitchen table—pennies, buttons, washers, and bottle caps.

Sticking a washer on the tip of his finger, Jayce said, "I thought you said your piggy bank was full."

Zeke pushed pop can tabs into a pile. "Yep!"

"This is nice stuff. Interesting stuff. But there's a difference between full and valuable."

Fishing out a nickel, the boy said, "Parts are money."

"Son." Jayce rubbed his chin and tried to explain. "Stores won't trade buttons for a chef coat."

"I know. But you and me could trade."

Ethan smiled crookedly as Jayce glanced between the boy and his treasures, then gave in. "How much for those two red checkers?"

DISSATISFACTORY ANSWER

onrad touched Ethan's shoulder. "Our captain wants to talk."

"To me?"

His mentor nodded. "I'll take your place here. He's waiting on the roof."

With one last look at his sleeping charge, Ethan obeyed.

He swept high toward glittering stars and pulled into a tight spiral that carried him back down to Tycho's side. Ethan landed and furled his wings. "I am here."

"How is Zeke?"

"All is as it should be."

His captain frowned, as if the answer dissatisfied him. "Young Guardian, you can call upon me at any time."

"I know it."

Tycho searched Ethan's face. "Do you?"

PROVISION AND PROTECTION

Tycho's challenge caught Ethan off guard. "Captain?"

"I was Sent to say this very thing, something I would have thought you knew," Tycho said, concern plain on his face. The tall archer extended the bow on which Ethan's name was carved. "You are under my watch-care. If you need me, call out. I will hear you, and I will fly to your aid."

"Thank you."

His captain sighed. "What is this about?"

"I cannot say for certain, but I can guess." Ethan smiled weakly. "In the near future, I will find myself in need, and you will be my help."

"This one?" asked Zeke, picking from the spinner's bottom row.

Grandma Nell glanced down. "Zinnias are perfect. But which color do you want? Blood red. Poison green. Royal purple."

"Wish I could get white ones and paint 'em." After careful scrutiny, he chose a multicolored variety with festive splatters and streaks. "Do they sell jungle vines?"

Ethan liked the mischievous sparkle in Nell's eyes.

"All kinds," she assured, reaching for scarlet runner beans and four-o-clocks.

People were quick to say that Zeke took after his father, but without a doubt, Jayce was his mother's son. Making Zeke a grandma's boy.

273
GOLDEN BIRTHDAY

On the sixth day of the sixth month, the Pomeroys celebrated Zeke's special day with a towering six-layer cake. Ethan enjoyed seeing his charge's excitement over marking the milestone. Apparently, it was a Big Deal, now needing *both* hands to reckon his age.

At the festivities' climax, Jayce announced, "A golden birthday only comes around once, so your mother and I made some extra special plans."

"I'm getting plans instead of presents?" asked Zeke.

His father grinned. "I've cleared my schedule. How does a camping trip sound?"

"When?"

"Starting tomorrow." Blue eyes sparkling, he added, "For six days."

Zeke whooped.

ℭampfire Songs

Three tents flanked the Pomeroys' campsite—one for Prissie and her mother, one for Tad and Neil, and one for the littler boys and their father. Their guardian angels fanned out through the surrounding woods, forming a much tighter perimeter than usual.

"Wingtip to wingtip," Alpheus murmured. "I'm sure we could reach."

"Agreed," whispered Ethan, who signaled Jomei. "Do you think your mentor would mind …?"

During evensong that first night, Trumble humored the eager apprentices. Rather than joining a wider perimeter, they crowded close. Wings outstretched. Gazes steady. Voices blending in celebration, the Hedge rejoiced to be so near.

275
HOME BASE

After an early morning fishing trip, Jayce and the two oldest boys prepped breakfast. Silvery scales. Fillet knives. Cast iron. While waiting for the fish to fry, Naomi passed out apples and oatmeal scotchies.

Zeke lured Jude aside and unwittingly sat at the feet of Ethan and Alpheus, who listened in on their whispered conference. "Soon as Momma says so, I'll show you the best parts," Zeke promised. "Places we didn't go see last time."

Jude nodded eagerly.

Gazing around with a proprietary air, the older brother declared, "For us, for now … this's home. Gotta know our way around!"

276
SPELUNKING

Ethan didn't care for the afternoon spent exploring the network of caves that spread beneath Sunderland State Park. No child of light liked spending time in such deep darkness. But where Zeke went, Ethan would follow. Wings outstretched. Eyes alert. Sword ready.

He and the other Guardians were ill-at-ease, but Ethan's discomfort turned to dread when a familiar whisper reached his ears. *"Prone to wander, prone to leave...."*

No one else seemed to have noticed Blight's sing-song greeting. Heart hammering, Ethan whispered, "Where are you?"

The demon's response sent a thrill of warning through the young warrior's soul.

"Familiar territory."

MISTER RANGER

As the spelunkers exited the caves, they passed a balding ranger keeping count. "… fourteen, fifteen, sixteen …." Piercing eyes met Ethan's over wire-rimmed glasses. "And one Guardian, slightly worse for wear."

"You are the Caretaker."

"And you're too pale," returned the disguised angel. "First time in the deep places?"

"Second. But … I heard something."

A gentle touch imparted comfort and calm. "Hardly surprising. Many lurk in the lower parts."

Gazing after Zeke, Ethan said, "I *must* keep him safe."

The ranger clasped his hands behind his back. "Trust what you can to me; trust the rest to God."

OTHER MISTER RANGER

While Zeke and Jude splashed around, a man paused to watch. Ethan's glance became a double-take. This must be the second Caretaker.

Zeke blurted, "Mister, are you an Indian?"

"At the moment, I'm a park ranger."

"Do you know stuff?"

"Knowing stuff is part of my job."

"Like what?"

"You're wading in Bear Creek. This tree is a red oak. And there are three deer watching you and your brother catch crayfish. If we sit here and hold very still, they'll come down for a drink."

Zeke's eyes widened. "You're mostly *amazing*!"

Dark eyes smiled. "Also part of my job."

Nature Scavenger Hunt

Zeke compared a sheet of paper with the items he'd spread on the ground. Ethan peered over his shoulder at the combination of simple words and pictures his mother had prepared. Tapping the list, the boy double-checked his progress, "Pine cone … twig … two kinds of leafs … a feather."

His "something rough" was a chunk of bark. A caterpillar was his "something fuzzy," kept safe inside the empty bottle that was his "something to recycle."

"Momma musta put this one on here for Prissie." Giving the last item a scowl, Zeke wondered, "Where'm I gonna find something *pink*?"

280
SOMETHING PINK

U p the ridge. Along the trails. Into the nature center. Through the picnic grounds. Ethan's long legs made it easy to keep up with the boy's quest. The Guardian didn't worry that Zeke had gone off on his own. The boy knew his way around the park almost as well as he knew his family's farm. But Ethan's steps faltered when Zeke reached the path running alongside the river.

Trees lined the banks, some leaning right out over the water. And from amidst the leaves of one, a dead branch jutted. That's where Blight perched. Waving a florescent pink Frisbee.

SHEATHED

Ethan was frantic to do something. Shout a warning. Grab hold and pull Zeke to safety. Or attack Blight, whose litany of encouragement accompanied the boy's climb.

But God stayed Ethan's hand with a word. *'Wait.'*

Although it broke his heart, the guardian angel sheathed his sword. Was this another time when his charge needed to taste the consequences of his actions? If so, he wouldn't do it alone. Unstrapping his sword, Ethan placed it on the ground beside Zeke's bag of scavenger hunt items and started to climb.

If Zeke went into danger, his Guardian would be with him.

282
In the Treetop

Zeke confidently swung up onto the branch where Blight had lodged his bait.

"Willingly, thrillingly," the demon chanted. "Foolishly, mulishly."

Ethan couldn't stop what had been set into motion, but Blight wouldn't have the last word. "Think, Zeke," he countered. "You do not need to win this game. The prize will not be worth the price."

The boy paused before stepping onto the barren limb. Glancing back, then down at the river below, he promised, "I'll hold on tight."

If only Ethan could make him understand. It doesn't matter how tenaciously you hold onto something if it's the *wrong* thing.

FRIGHTENED

Ethan's heart clenched as Zeke ignored common sense and better judgment. Fixing his eyes on the pink Frisbee, the boy stretched for it but came up short. So he shimmied out further.

Blight's glee lent a malicious sparkle to his eyes. He jostled the dead limb in time with his taunting. "Bend the bough, and break the bond."

A sudden *crack* stole the color from Zeke's face. The limb sagged beneath him, and he cast a wild look back toward safety. In that instant, Ethan felt certain that Zeke's gaze locked with his.

And then his precious boy whispered, "Help?"

284
TORN APART

With a resounding *snap*, the branch broke, and Zeke vanished into the river. Ethan's whole being vibrated with a longing to follow, but God had not released him. He needed to wait.

Blight turned to him with a sly smile. "Follow, and you Fall. Stay, and your service ends. Either way, you're free … *friend.*"

Zeke surfaced, floundering against the undercurrent. Ethan glanced around, but the path along the river was empty, and the Caretakers weren't in sight. Zeke needed a miracle. But his life was in God's hands. "I will wait," Ethan whispered.

'Child of light, you may go.'

Ethan flung himself down, using a quick wingbeat to lend speed to his plunge. The river was wide and deep and dark, but the young Guardian didn't need to see. When an angel is Sent, he always knows the way.

Kicking through rushing undercurrents, Ethan reached out. His knuckles bumped a sneaker; his fingertips brushed an elbow. Righting the boy, Ethan pulled him against his chest as he carried him out of danger. Zeke's arms locked around his neck as they broke the surface. While choking for breath, Zeke nearly throttled his rescuer. But Ethan didn't mind. Not at all.

No Swimming

"Fear not. I have you."

Zeke's stranglehold tightened. If it weren't for the buoying effect of Ethan's outspread wings, the boy would have pulled them back under.

Ethan stroked his charge's matted hair. "You are safe. I am with you."

"'Kay."

Just as Ethan maneuvered to the riverbank, the younger of the two Caretakers paddled over in a yellow kayak. "Gentlemen, swimming is prohibited in the river. I thought you knew that, Zeke."

The boy's head popped up. "I wasn't swimmin' … least not too good. I fell."

"Then it's a good thing my friend saw you. Zeke, meet Ethan."

Blue eyes focused on Ethan's face, and the young warrior blinked. He hadn't been expecting an introduction. Zeke looked ready to say something, but a fit of coughing interrupted him. And the coughing turned into sobs. Ethan tried to bring his wings around in order to comfort his precious boy.

Except Ranger Prentice's hand landed on his shoulder.

And the Guardian realized several things. His wings were gone. So was his armor. And he was barefoot. And wearing khaki shorts and a pink T-shirt.

The Caretaker offered him a pair of flip-flops and said, "I'll do most of the talking."

Strangely Familiar

Ranger Prentice draped a striped towel around the boy's shoulders and roughed up is hair. "Calm down, Zeke."

"Fear not," Ethan repeated. His humming gradually lapsed into his favorite lullaby for the boy.

When Zeke wiped his nose on his rescuer's shoulder, the ranger produced a handkerchief.

Sniffle. *Honk*. And a hard stare. Zeke asked, "How come I know that song?"

"I cannot say."

"How come I know *you*?"

"Perhaps we are friends."

"Okay." Zeke's brows drew down, and he announced, "You talk funny."

Ethan blinked. "I do?"

With a little pat, Zeke generously said, "S'okay. It's like the Bible."

"We'll bring you to your family," Padgett offered.

Zeke squirmed. "I want Daddy, but …."

"But?" prompted the ranger.

Zeke wrinkled his nose. "I think I'm in trouble."

"No," soothed Ethan. "Your father will welcome you with gladness."

A sidelong glance. A sigh. A nod. But as soon as Ethan took a step toward the Pomeroys' campsite, Zeke blurted, "Wait! My scavenger stuff!"

Ranger Prentice glanced questioningly at Ethan, who chuckled. "Is the game still important?"

"If I get back first, imma win. On account of I found something pink!"

Ethan plucked self-consciously at his sodden T-shirt. "So you did."

290
GENEROSITY

Ethan had been frantic, yet now he was in a state of flustered bliss. Zeke was in his arms. Seeing him. Talking to him. Nonstop.

"It's like a treasure hunt," the boy rambled. "But a race, too. Neil mostly wins. 'Cept I think Tad lets him. The prize is a *whole* cake. You like cake?"

"I am uncertain."

"How come?"

Ethan had no idea how to answer.

"Aint'cha tasted cake?"

"No, but it smells good."

"Yep! 'Specially mine. Want me to make you one?"

With a sheepish glance at Ranger Prentice, Ethan admitted, "That would only add to my joy."

A Miracle Named Ethan

"But thankfully, Ethan was in the right place at the right time," Ranger Prentice explained.

The young warrior relinquished his charge into Naomi's arms, then shuffled his feet self-consciously.

Jayce shook his stunned expression first and offered a firm handshake. "Thank you, Ethan."

"Fear not," he murmured, gazing down at the man. "Your son is safe."

Naomi passed Zeke to Jayce before throwing her arms around Ethan, hugging him fiercely. "Thank God you were there!"

He glanced at Lucan, who waved encouragingly. Swallowing hard, Ethan touched her shoulder and said, "I also thank God. His timing was good."

OUR HERO

The Pomeroys provided their hero with a seat by the campfire, and Jayce began a round of wholly unnecessary introductions. Ethan wished he could relay clever little messages as Milo had once done, but he was entirely tongue-tied.

Tad shook his hand.

Neil bluntly asked, "Did you save my little brother's life?"

"I did my part."

The teen hurried off and brought his own blanket. Wrapping it around Ethan's shoulders, Neil murmured, "Thanks."

Next came Beau. The tenderhearted boy's pale face and shy hug made Ethan miss his wings. Sharing the warmth of his blanket, the Guardian whispered, "Fear not."

The More the Merrier

"Can I keep him?"

Jayce chuckled. "Sure, sure. If your Momma says so."

Zeke grinned up at Ethan, whose lap he'd claimed as his throne. One he willingly shared with Jude. "Momma says more's merry!"

Ethan wasn't used to this much attention. His whole Flight had arrived, and Garrick and Yannis were making faces. Alpheus looked on with a tender expression. Conrad smirked. Verrill plucked "Kumbaya" on his harp. Only Tycho remained alert and restless.

When the Flight captain realized Ethan was staring, he strode over and leaned down to murmur, "Things are stirring, and I am Sent. To you."

The Food of Angels

At her mother's prompting, Zeke's sister invited Ethan to join them for dinner.

"May I?" he asked, glancing to Conrad for reassurance. His mentor's smirk widened into a smile.

Prissie nodded. "Zeke *wants* you to stay. Obviously."

The boy insisted on being Ethan's personal chef for the evening. Neil joked, "Hope you have a taste for char!"

Tad smile sympathetically. "Don't worry. Zeke hasn't *fully* incinerated anything since *last* summer."

"Marked improvement," agreed Jayce.

And so later on, Ethan graciously accepted a hot dog with flaking black skin, smothered in mustard. His first taste of human food burned his tongue.

Dark brought out the fireflies … and the marshmallows. Zeke presented his latest creation. "I can't bake a cake here, but I make good s'mores."

A nibble. A smile. "It is sweet."

Zeke explained, "The names a mush of *some* and *more*. Because once you have one, you always want s'more!"

Ethan's smile wobbled.

The boy noticed and whispered, "Whassa matter?"

"I will miss this."

Zeke's brows drew together. "Are you goin' away?"

"Not far," Ethan promised.

"Can you visit?"

"I cannot say."

"That usually means *no*," Zeke grumbled.

Ethan gently mussed the boy's hair. "It only means *be patient*."

Flip Flop

Goodbyes lingered, but Ranger Prentice finally escorted Ethan away. He expected a transformational touch, but Padgett didn't undo the Guardian's disguise. Instead, he pointed southwest. "Walk home."

Ethan looked down at himself. "Like this?"

With a small shrug, the other angel said, "It's only a few miles."

Through the woods. Past a ridge. Into an open field. With the soft slap of unfamiliar sandals, Ethan aimed for the boundary he'd often patrolled. Without armor, weapon, or wings, he felt vulnerable, but red and turquoise sparks rode the night breezes high overhead. Tonight, his mentor and captain were his guardian angels.

STRANGELY DIM

Once Ethan entered the long rows of apple trees, Blight stepped into his path. "My friend, why are you suddenly dim? The glory of heaven is gone from your face."

The young Guardian didn't flinch from the demon's curiosity … or his touch.

Blight whispered, "Taking on the form of a man …?"

Catching the demon's wrist, Ethan shook his head. "I am neither friend nor savior."

Instead of pulling away, Blight stepped closer. "What then? For I *know* you are mine."

"Yes, I *am* Sent to you." Ethan stole the blade from the demon's sash. "To be your jailor."

CATCH AND KEEP

Blight nodded. "I accept your offer."

Ethan set the dagger's edge against Blight's throat. "You have no choice."

With a slowly growing smile, he countered, "The blade is dull. As are your wits. *You* are the one without a choice. Sent to me, with me you *must* remain." He lowered his voice. "I win."

At Ethan's call, Tycho and Conrad spiraled to his aid.

"*Inside* the Hedge?" asked Conrad in sharp tones.

Tycho reached for Blight, but the demon ducked under the archer's hand. To Ethan's mortification, Blight took shelter behind him, saying, "*He* caught me. *He* shall keep me."

Front Lawn

A small Hedge bristled around Blight, who smiled at the gathered Guardians and used his jailor for a shield. Ethan would have preferred to distance himself, but his Sending was clear.

The silver-haired ranger arrived then, his uniform traded for shining raiment. Ethan dragged Blight out from behind his back, and the Caretaker said, "Choose your prison."

"I know a place. Close. Quiet. Seal me there."

Blight sounded confident, but Ethan felt him tremble. Pity vanished the moment he realized Blight was laughing. The demon's farewell was a whispered warning. "Keep me well, or I'll catch you next ... *friend.*"

300
Enter into Joy

Two Messengers found Ethan alone. "The blight is gone from the orchard," declared Verrill. "Well done, good and Faithful servant."

"Yes, but …." Ethan tugged at his pink T-shirt. "That Caretaker forgot to change me back."

Raz laughed. Verrill tutted. Padgett arrived.

Returned to his former glory, Ethan flew straight into one little boy's dream.

Zeke collided with the warrior's embrace. "You're here!"

"Yes. I am with you."

"Like always." Zeke muttered, "I 'member *now*, 'cept I mostly forget."

"Do you mind?"

"Nah. S'good."

Ethan agreed heartily and mushed all his feelings into that same joyous, boyish monosyllable. "S'good."

ALSO BY
CHRISTA KINDE

THRESHOLD SERIES

The Blue Door (Book 1)
The Hidden Deep (Book 2)
The Broken Window (Book 3)
The Garden Gate (Book 4)

THRESHOLD COMPANION STORIES

Angels All Around
Angels in Harmony
Angels on Guard
Angel on High
Angel Unaware
Rough and Tumble
Tried and True
Sage and Song

*Angels: A 90-Day Devotional
about God's Messengers*

Ten years after the events of *The Blue Door*, Prissie Pomeroy experiences an angelic reprise.

PURSUING PRISSIE

CHAPTER 1
THE USUAL THINGS

When the Faithful gather, it's usually for song, but the six angels in the Pomeroys' hayloft stood silent. Boots scuffed the straw-littered floor. Fingers tapped a restless rhythm. Expressions were easy to read. Confusion marked both apprentice Guardians. Their mentors were concerned, and their respective captains were at a loss how to comfort them.

Jedrick tried first. "This is not the first time Miss Pomeroy has been at the center of mysterious ways."

Tamaes's flame-hued wings trembled with emotions his voice didn't betray. "While that is true, this is unusual in the extreme. *Prissie* is my charge."

Taweel grunted. "Show Jedrick."

Obeying his mentor, Tamaes extended a large, sun-browned hand. Letters etched their way across his palm in heaven's language, spelling out a name—*Hezekiah Pomeroy*.

"Her brother," Jedrick mused aloud, his gaze switching to a Guardian with pearlescent pink wings. "*Your* charge."

"Zeke," confirmed Ethan. Although the bristle-haired angel was clearly the youngest of their gathering, he seemed to be taking this new Sending in stride. With an apologetic air, he offered his palm. Proof of his altered status showed against fair skin—*Priscilla Pomeroy*.

"An interesting trade-off," remarked Conrad, who mentored Ethan. "Any idea why two Guardians would be asked to switch places?"

Tycho, the tall archer who captained the Flight to which Conrad and Ethan belonged, asked, "Have either of these children done anything unusual?"

Taweel snorted.

"*Lately*?" Tycho amended.

Tamaes rubbed at the letters on his hand. "Prissie's days have been quiet. She stays busy." In a gentler tone, he added, "She misses us."

Ethan shrugged. "Unless football practice and profiteroles are newly added to the perils we guard against, Zeke's days are also quiet. For him."

"Meaning they aren't," Conrad said.

Fondness warmed Ethan's tone. "Zeke is Zeke."

Jedrick folded muscular arms across his breastplate. "Since the siblings both reside here and work together, you will often remain close to the one whose name is on your heart. But with this changing of the guard, your first responsibility must be the one whose name is on your hand."

Tamaes's wry smile tugged at the scar running down the side of his face. "I look forward to the challenge."

Ethan touched Tamaes's forearm and warned, "Zeke still pulls stunts."

"Prissie still watches for miracles," Tamaes

confided.

"He means well."

"She trusts too easily."

"He never stops."

"She always hopes."

Ethan tipped his head to one side, catching the more bashful Guardian's gaze. "Zeke *will* stretch your wings to their limits."

Clasping the younger warrior's hand, Tamaes said, "And your wings will delight Prissie."

Folds of translucent pink shimmered in the dim loft. Ethan bemusedly said, "Her favorite color has long been established, but she is unlikely to see them."

Tamaes shook his head. "She will. Be ready."

PURSUING PRISSIE
A POMEROY FAMILY LEGACY NOVEL

ISBN 978-1-63123-016-5 (e-book)
ISBN 978-1-63123-028-8 (print edition)